MOON X

JOHN P. WARREN

AS FAR AS COULD BE SEEN, THERE were cornfields surrounding the oasis of a small futuristic city that seemed aberrant in this setting. This town, populated by over five hundred thousand people, had ultra-modern buildings, advanced infrastructure, and at night, was lit up by seemingly natural light. Light with a fragrance of delicacy not formed by electrical currents but more flowing like liquid. The buildings that this light used at night were polygonal-shaped and constructed of a form of glass.

Three elderly people, dressed in white robes, went about their duties consisting of breeding recording, controlled marriages, and other civic activities. Two new couples made their way inside Administrator Gladstone's building, called the Capitol, the tallest in the town and the government and engineering headquarters. He could be described as the father of the colony, and it was he who determined which couples would qualify for these arranged marriages. He was aged 57. As the two couples came inside his office, he stood over them and examined them like a doctor would. Once satisfied with their vitals, he placed a hi-tech head-piece on each of their heads.

A woman known simply as Madame Official entered. She

assisted Gladstone in the selection process. Gladstone rushed back to his desk and checked a virtual schematic of the first couple's brains. An expression of frustration consumed his face. "Why? Why?"

He turned to Madame Official. "Get those off them!"

To the couple, he swore, "Get out! Get out! You're not counterparts! You're nowhere close!"

Gladstone followed the couple to the doors and slammed them shut from the inside as the couple left his office. He signaled to the second couple to leave too. He viciously grabbed Madame Official and yelled, "Get Fielding!"

She moved over to a console that emitted light and made a waving gesture with her hands. Fielding's virtual facial image sprang up from the center of the console. "Madame Official! Let me guess, not compatible?"

"Administrator Gladstone wishes to see you now."

"Does he?"

Fielding entered Gladstone's office, somewhat troubled. If he found out what he was really up to, then he'd be a dead man. "I know!" Fielding said.

"Know what?"

"I had you under investigation. I have evidence that you're getting couples ready for them!"

"So?" Gladstone laughed grandiosely.

"I want you to know that I won't allow you to get away with this!"

Gladstone simpered an arrogant smirk. "Oh yeah? Just how are you going to stop me or prevent the inevitable, Fielding?"

"I have followers, support. I'm not alone!"

"Only for your usefulness would I have eliminated you long since. I'll make this suggestion to you – don't make me expedite matters."

Fielding walked out of Gladstone's office without closing the door, a sure sign of disrespect toward him.

It was a few hours later in this complex, and Fielding had snuck into the Capitol, luckily without being noticed by Gladstone's diligent guards. He crept into a large room – a DNA library of genetic capsules, each housing unformed human clones. Fielding was now at his desired destination. He appeared to be manipulating one particular clone. He began working frantically on a console where the human DNA helix sprung up in a virtual image beside him. "This is my insurance policy, Gladstone. My legacy..." he muttered to himself.

He continued for a moment and then paused. "There..."

He then switched off the console, which made a loud tone enough to alert someone, and the image of the DNA helix vanished. He was about to leave when Gladstone came inside. "What are you doing down here, Fielding?"

"Just getting my evidence ready."

"That better be all it is."

Gladstone turned his back to Fielding, who seemed increasingly nervous and was standing behind him. Gladstone reached inside his jacket pocket and pulled out a dagger. He turned around to Fielding and pushed it into his chest. Fielding fell to the floor. "Any final words?" he asked him with a sadistic grin.

Fielding was struggling to speak but managed barely enough to utter his final words, "... Someday... you will know my... legacy..."

He managed to push a button attached to his belt. A distortion surrounded him, and as he began to vanish, rage and disdain consumed Gladstone. "Search everywhere for him. I want that obscenity found!"

Gladstone entered a trance like state. His eyes lit up and shone brightly with blue light as if there were LED bulbs in his eye sockets. He could only utter something sounding like, "Yes, Master. I will find him. Our plans will not be thwarted."

Fielding was somewhere else in a large room. There was equipment arranged everywhere. He immediately rushed over to a computer console, and a small transparent force field appeared. He gazed at it with marvel and picked up a small hand-sized console, activating it. Inside this chamber, surrounded by the transparent force field, a small sphere of light emerged. Fielding smiled to himself with growing satisfaction.

CHAPTER 1

RIVERS TOWN, New Hampshire, was your average North American sleepy small town. It got its name from the two rivers that meet into a third one. Nothing outrageous ever happened here until today when there were a small number of people going about their daily lives, particularly a young couple named James and Nadia. They shared a kiss when Nadia saw, in the corner of her eye, a strange-looking man lying on the sidewalk. He was wearing a white garment, aged twenties/early thirties, and his expressionless face scared her somewhat. She couldn't help but think how incongruent he seemed like a freshwater fish suddenly placed in a humid desert. He was weird and looked weird to everybody watching. She thought this man was not in the certain kind of harmony which other people were with the world.

This man stood upright and tried to begin walking down Main Street slowly. He soon fell to the ground helplessly and tried to stand up to no avail. Nadia gestured to her boyfriend to go over to him to help. Others gathered around him too. Each was alerted, wondering where this strange young man came from. Nadia turned to James, "Is he alive?" she asked with sincere empathy toward the stranger.

"Call a doctor! Now!" James replied.

Nadia took out her cell phone and began dialling for help.

"Operator! A man needs urgent attention! We need an ambulance straight away! Main Street! Now!"

The stranger didn't appear to be responding to James's attempts to revive him. "He doesn't seem to be coming around. Does anybody know him?"

"I've never seen him before today," an old woman replied.

Nadia noticed something written on the right-hand side of his garment. She quickly turned to James, "I think there's something printed here. It's in English. I think his name is *Seth*."

James began to slap Seth lightly on each side of his face. "Help is coming. The paramedics are on their way."

More of Rivers Town's folk converged around the vicinity. James grabbed Nadia's hand to interrupt her consternating concern. "Get someone to get me towels and water."

He noticed a rash on Seth's leg that wasn't present earlier. "What has happened to him? Where did he come from?"

"He's sure not from around here," replied Nadia, a little scared.

The welcoming sound of an ambulance siren could be heard, much to the relief of everybody present, Nadia. "Oh, thank God."

The other onlookers began to move out of the way to allow the paramedics to do their work. They placed Seth, who was now subdued, on a trolley and soon brought him off to hospital.

Nadia couldn't stop her sobbing tears that fell from her eyes. She had a bad feeling about all this and couldn't stop a discomforting feeling throughout her body. The strangeness of this man wandering down Main Street, this man simply known as Seth was enough to give her peculiar sensations. James on the other hand was indifferent to Seth and what he would represent. All he cared for was the date night they had planned together and now was beginning to resent this stranger that somehow infected their normal ordinary routine of a young couple's life.

Later, that evening and much to James's irritation and growing frustration, Nadia canceled their date night activities. She left his apartment without telling her boyfriend to where she was heading to. That place was Rivers Town General Hospital. She was about to fetch her bicycle when James stormed out of the apartment. "Nadia! Where are you going? I have a nice meal cooked, your favorite, beef stroganoff and that movie I purchased online to cuddle up together on the sofa."

Nadia ignored him and his calls until he rushed over and grabbed her arm. She was about to hop on the bicycle. James pulled that away from her too. "Stop it, James!"

"What's going on, Nadia? Oh, I see. You're off to the hospital to check on that drunk or hobo or whatever they like to be called nowadays."

"I am really concerned for his wellbeing. Don't you think that we somehow have to watch out for him since we are the ones who first found him like that on the street?" cried Nadia.

James shook his head and rolled his eyes. "One of the most endearing things I find about you, honey, is the way you put other people first but I'm telling you that I need you now. Screw Seth. He's at the hospital. What more do you need?"

"You're so damned selfish at times, you know that?"

"Fine! Go to him. See if I'm bothered about him. I couldn't care less whether he lives or dies!"

Nadia took her bicycle and cycled as fast as humanly possible to the hospital. When she arrived there, she wasted no time and stormed into reception demanding to know the health status of the stranger.

An oddly composed man came over to reception and grabbed her by the arm. "What is your relationship to this man called Seth?"

"Let me go!"

He clenched her arm, hurting her. "Answer the question!"

"Alright! Alright!"

He released her arm.

"Me and my boyfriend called the ambulance to bring him here."

"Do you know him, or do you know where he came from?" this man asked.

"No, we never saw him before today. Can I see him, please?"

"You certainly may not."

Nadia was about to plead with this man who seemed to be some kind of security personnel. She simpered the words only he watched her lips as he predicted she would pursue the matter and shouted, "Don't bother! Leave here now or I'll call the police!"

She left the hospital humbly and retreated to her boyfriend's apartment. On her way she noticed a funny cloud formation that seemed prophetic and mulled over the events of the day and evening that was. She determined everything that occurred was indeed something profound.

This ominous event gripped this town, and little did any of its population know at this point that something significant was about to happen soon. Certain people in Rivers Town would play an important role in trying to come to terms with a global quandary that would affect every man, woman, and child.

CHAPTER 2

JUST ANOTHER DAY as our solemn and pale moon orbited planet Earth as usual, with man-made satellites carrying out their automated functions and the sun basking the world with its warm sunshine. All these celestial bodies, if sentient, would be oblivious to the chaos, war, and poverty taking place below the clouds.

This fraction of a moment in a seemingly serene state of cosmic bliss was about to face a contradiction, though. A distortion in space, about three-quarters the distance between the moon and Earth, erupted. At the boundaries of time, space, and the realm outside these, a new, second moon emerged. It differed from its sister, our moon, far from being innocuous. It appeared vengeful and dark, as if a cataclysmic event had just taken place, and was twice the size of our moon. Its now charcoaled terrain and atmosphere were destroyed.

In New York City, cars crashed. People heard the raucous, thunderous eruption in the sky and looked up with senses of marvel, panic, and fear to witness this new moon emerging from nothingness as it cradled in the blue sky. This scene was repeated worldwide as governments declared martial law, and the world's population pondered if this event marked the end of everything as they once knew it. The United States Army arrived on streets across the nation to quell protesters and looters. Christian religious leaders saw it as a harbinger of the second coming of Christ, while other faiths viewed it along similar lines. The media dubbed this second moon as Moon X.

In New York City, Rick Sanchez was just staring up at the sky, inebriated. He had drunk so much that afternoon that he thought he was imagining things when he saw the second moon in the sky. His police car opened, and a scantily dressed hooker got inside and sat in the passenger's seat. "Rick, are you gonna tie me up in those handcuffs again?"

"Wait, I think my mind's giving in. I'm seeing a second moon in the goddamn sky!"

"Trust me, baby, it's not your head giving in. It's really there!"

"I've got to get sober. Another time, eh, Candy? Rick said, as if he couldn't care less about future liaisons with Candy."

He stared up at the new turbulent moon and something struck him. It was an oddity like him now, like what he had become which was a wasted cop filling in the hours to earn a living only he was doing anything but living. He disharmonised with society some time back after a personal loss. Failure was something he never did but now he excelled in it. His concentration was broken when heard Candy speak to him in that irritating, squeaky voice which he grew to despise. "Okay, but just remember you owe me for this call out or better still go to your high-class call girl in D.C.!"

Rick then realized he must have at some point told her about his newfound affection for someone else. He dismissed what she just said and put it down to rivalry or perhaps plain jealously and didn't react. She got out of the police car, slamming the door shut quite angrily and then Rick's phone rang.

"Sanchez, we want you back. Report to me in DC ASAP!"

"Hayes?" Rick said to himself. "Just what in the hell's going on?"

"Have you seen what's up there in the sky doing a little dance with the sun and our normal moon?"

"It looks like a smaller moon. Don't tell me all those investigations you did have somehow caused this situation?"

"It's nothing like we've ever encountered before. Get your ass in my office this time tomorrow, understood, Sanchez?"

This was like a nightmare for Rick. On one hand he knew that he was the best man they got. On the other, he was in no fit state to go back. All that was going through his mind was finding an excuse as Hayes yelled down the phone to him to get his act together was to tell him to fuck off and leave him be. "I can't do this, Hayes!" cried Rick.

Hayes shot up from his desk on the other side of the call and kicked his chair to one side in a venomous fit of rage. "Damnit, Rick! Stop fucking every hooker when a sniff of them come your way. Get sober and smarten up or else we're all screwed! I need you, Sanchez. You're the best we got!"

Rick pondered for a moment and thought how fucked up this world was and how life cruel as it had screwed him over more than once. At times he couldn't care less about the world's fate. It fucked him over and he wanted to do the same. However hateful and vengeful he felt, a shred of decency began to shine at the core of his soul and grew brighter with every passing second. It could only be he who could solve this mystery and save the world from annihilation. That made him feel special again as if he more than just counted. He now had a new purpose, his old job back. This combined with a new sense of self value and this value reflected toward humanity he once cared about inspired him to think differently.

One day later, Rick Sanchez was sober and back at his post. Hayes had called him to attend a high-level meeting with the Secretary of Defense, Robert Spence. He made his way to Section-S HQ, where Hayes gave a briefing to Spence. Rick entered the briefing room to find Hayes, two men, and a woman he hadn't seen before. They were Spence's people. He sat down, and they waited, clearing their throats in succession. Minutes later, the doors opened, and the Secretary of Defense entered. Spence, sharply dressed in a suit and carrying his briefcase, gestured for them to sit back down rather aggressively. He didn't respond well to formalities, something he had in common with Hayes. The first man greeted the Secretary, and Spence asked, "Did this moon come from another dimension or alternate reality, or did the entire body come from deep in the past or the distant future?"

"No. We strongly believe it's a small planet, a planetoid. Judging by the energy released to conceal it, it must have been cloaked for centuries," the second man replied.

"You're telling me that this 'planetoid' has always been here?"

"Yes. Its gravitational pull and magnetic energy had no effect on the Earth's oceans. They were camouflaged too."

"Why now? Is there a threat of an alien invasion?"

The woman interjected, "They may be dying and wish to seek our help."

Spence became deeply concerned. "Look, Kimberly, I don't like this one bit. The President is going to keep the state of martial law in effect."

"You're the Secretary of Defense, what do you think?" she asked.

"I don't believe in little green men, and I'm not going to allow anything heinous to happen to our world. I want everything that was analysed by Section-S on extraterrestrial matters. Who is in charge now?"

Hayes nodded. "I am, sir. I was a former NYPD Commissioner. My name is Brian Hayes, and I was recently appointed in charge of Section-S."

Hayes was about to introduce Rick to Spence when Kimberly interjected once again, "Sir, Section-S doesn't have the funding or expertise to find out what's going on here. You said yourself that you don't believe in 'little green men'."

"So, you're saying I'm the reason why it is inept?" Spence replied.

She became mortified, "Not quite, sir. It's just smoke and mirrors."

"Alright, alright! I'll give them whatever resources they need. In the meantime, let's keep the population under control. Hayes, I want you to find out what's going on up there?!"

He got up and left. Hayes and Rick stood up. The two men and woman didn't utter a word. They got up too and left. Hayes turned to Rick. "Just our luck! I thought this was gonna be an easy ride, until that damned second moon appeared in the sky, and now we are the ones entrusted by the Secretary of Defense to find out how and where it came from?"

"I'm sure we'll find out soon enough."

"Of course."

CHAPTER 3

THE WASHINGTON MONUMENT obelisk stood true and noble, set against the now placid, dusky sky. In the affluent suburbs, reeking of opulence and social stature, was the apartment of Sandra O'Toole. The lights were dimmed, and they were having a romantic evening dinner with red wine in their home. She was Rick's exclusive call girl, although he didn't truly believe that was the case. Now that he was back in Washington, D.C., he could visit her more often.

Rick had met her about five years ago, about a year after he lost his wife to leukaemia. Their instant attraction and suitable compatibility became evident; in other words, they became besotted with each other, and it was sure true love their "relationship" was built upon. "How many times have you tried now to book us into that Creole restaurant downtown, and they're always booked up?"

Rick smiled. He knew she wasn't digging at him in a nagging way, but sort of commencing flirtation. "Isn't this much better? I told you that I *can* cook."

"A master of many trades, Agent Rick Sanchez. Just what exactly is Section-S?"

"The FBI's Special branch for the paranormal, UFO sightings, not to mention supposed alien abductions!" Sounds like the reject cases to me."

"That's what I get for asking you a stupid question – I forgot your work is classified. Another glass of wine?"

Rick nodded, and Sandra stood up, poured him another glass, and moved amorously over to him. She stroked his strong arms and shaven head as they embraced and kissed. He rubbed his fingers along her straight brown hair. They both became aroused by each other's fondlings.

Sandra pulled Rick gently towards their bedroom, and she removed her clothing, as did he. They kissed passionately. A few minutes later, they were being intimate in the biblical sense and were writhing in pleasure when a tiny sphere of light appeared out of nowhere near the bed. The couple was much too busy enjoying each other to notice. This tiny sphere of light penetrated Sandra's stomach. She flinched with minor discomfort. Rick had his eyes closed, not noticing anything strange. They continued.

Afterward, Rick was thinking to himself how special this experience was with Sandra, even if he wasn't going to admit it to her right away. He was drowsy and lapsed into a state of sleep, where he dreamt of his wife long before his time with Sandra. Her name was Rebecca. She was the opposite of Sandra, not just with her long blonde hair and being much taller, but she knew Rick much better than Sandra did, as they met in Section-S in Washington, D.C.

Rick, in his dream, was back on the night before he got married to Rebecca, remembering as if he was reliving these moments of nervousness and self-doubt about being a good husband to her. He thought on that night what a very lucky man he was to have such a beautiful woman like Rebecca take him in marriage and how he owed all to her. Ever since her passing, he had become lost, with days filled with half-assed attempts at solving cases in the NYPD and weekend nights usually seeking solace with call girls in cheap motels. He was by no means a dirty cop, just an apathetic one.

Suddenly, in his dream, he was at the church on his wedding day, and the organ was playing when the doors opened, and a silhouette of Rebecca began walking down the aisle, then he awoke with cruel abruptness. Sadness and anger filled his mind. He felt like screaming out for her, only his senses were drawn to the smell of Sandra cooking breakfast in her kitchen. He immediately got up and dressed himself.

"Not going already? You worked up quite an appetite last night."

"I really have to. I have to report back at my old post. I don't want to run late."

"Let's hope there's no little green men going to jump down from that new moon up there."

"Sandra, this is no joke. We don't know what Moon X means, but I'm going to find out."

"And if you don't, Rick? What next? You'll keep drinking and bed-hopping? This is not the way to handle things!"

"Lately, it's the only way I know, and besides, I'm not the one who's chosen a certain profession – bed-hopping!"

Sandra flung one of the plates she was about to put some crispy bacon on and exclaimed, "Fuck you, Rick! It's only you!"

Rick grinned sarcastically, "If I could only place my faith in that. Prove it to me. Let me the only one because I want to take you somewhere today."

"What? Really?"

"Yes."

Sandra, taken aback asked, "But, let me ask you, Rick Sanchez, What faith have you in me? I really hope you find your way back in more ways than one on your expedition to whatever you discover with that Moon X!"

With that said, Rick decided there and then that it was his cue to get the hell out of her apartment. He was already late and smelt post-coital. He pressed the remote key control, opened his car door with fury, and got inside. This was a typical beginning to a typical Rick Sanchez Day, no matter where he was living. He pondered, *what's the use?*

Then he realized that life was much too short. "Please, Sandra. Let me show you I'm serious."

She smiled back to him as she followed him outside. "Where are you taking me?"

"We don't have much time. Just come with me in my car and you will see."

Sandra got inside Rick's car, and he drove outside of the city. He kept quiet all through the journey. Sandra knew it was futile in pestering him to where he was taking her. They arrived at his desired location. It was a small chapel.

Sandra was slightly intimated in a pleasant way and wondered as to why he brought her here. "A church, Rick? Why?"

"You're Catholic, I'm Catholic. Let's seal the deal?"

"What?" she replied, incredulous to what he was asking of her. "You mean marriage? You want to marry me today?"

Rick smiled sincerely. "Yes, Sandra. I do."

"Why?" she asked, not knowing if this was one of his pranks or not.

"Because I love you, Sandra. Ever since Moon X appeared and when Hayes convinced me to come back to Section-S, I found my purpose in life again. I'm no longer pissed off with the world or the negative things that happened in my life. I value my life now and I value you, enough to share my life with you."

"Yes! I will marry you, Rick Sanchez!" Sandra said with glee and delight as if she was a high school girl being asked to the prom.

"I have filed the paperwork, and I gave notice to the priest. Considering it could be the end of days and all, well, let's just say he was more than willing to accommodate us today."

"Today?" Sandra asked.

"Right now."

"Let's do it!"

Rick and Sandra went inside to the church and met Father Flanagan. He was an elderly Irish priest and married them an hour later.

CHAPTER 4

AT RIVERS TOWN GENERAL HOSPITAL, Seth was lying on the bed, linked to a monitor and with a tube down his throat. He was conscious, with his eyes open. The chief doctor, known as Doctor Snowdon, arrived and was accompanied by two female nurses. He was a tall figure, wearing a grey suit and had wavy silver hair to accompany his long face. He spoke harmoniously with velvet tones as he peered over Seth's chart attached to the bed. He raised an eyebrow, turned to the nurses, and said in a sotto voce, "He is awake; however, time will tell if he's lucid."

He then moved over to the monitor to check its readings. Seth began to raise his right hand and became agitated. Snowdon was startled and said to the nurses with an air of authority, "You need to sedate him better!"

He then faced Seth. "Please try to relax, sir. You're in a serious situation regarding your well-being. Nurse, inject him now!"

She applied the syringe to Seth's hip. He fell asleep within moments and now remained menacingly silent. This unsettled Snowdon a lot, and he became fearful of what he represented. "He has lesions that could only have been caused by exposure to massive levels of radiation. There isn't any nuclear power plant within a radius of seven hundred miles. No way could he last that long! Our friend here has a lot of explaining to do when he wakes up!" He said to the nurses.

Snowdon gestured to the nurses to leave, and he took out his cell phone to call a man called Lucini. He was in charge of the mortuary and wanted to see Seth for himself, to scrutinize him, and to witness the oddity he was. Lucini always found that people who were in some way inferior to him made him feel more secure and better about himself. He arrived at Snowdon's office, eager. Snowdon was downing a Scotch and was becoming increasingly nervous about this entire situation. Lucini sneered at Snowdon behind his back with somewhat hostility. He knew he was uncharacteristically losing a grip on things, which pleased him somewhat.

"He's from that second moon, isn't he, Lucini?" Snowdon said, scared.

"We don't know that. There could be another, rational explanation."

"This doesn't look good!"

And as Snowdon uttered those words, Seth rose up, pulled the tubes that were stuck in him out, and went over to Lucini. He reacted to this unwanted stranger and tried to restrain him, only for Seth to reach out, pinning him to the wall. Snowdon was speechless when he saw that Seth had him raised very high up indeed from the floor. Lucini became scared like a cowardly bully. "Please, let me go!"

Seth let him drop onto his ass. "You think that you can treat me like some lab experiment? I will not be poked and prodded again."

Snowdon quickly regained his composure and made a gesture with his hands for Seth to be seated back on the bed. "Nobody's going to hurt you, Seth. I am a doctor, and I wish to only help you."

Seth became saddened at what he'd just heard. "You can't help me. She's gone."

"Who's gone?" asked Snowdon in a manipulative tone.

"Never mind, it's all useless now."

Lucini got up from the ground, fretful. Snowdon gave him a look as if he should have known better.

Snowdon pompously moved over to Seth. "If you don't allow me to treat you, then you will die. You've suffered severe radiation poisoning. You should be dead; however, your body has remarkable healing power. I've never seen anything like it before."

"You know where I come from?" Seth nervously asked.

Snowdon nodded, smiling mischievously. "And that means that you are one very unique, special individual indeed."

He went over to a nearby table and opened up a box. In it was a large syringe, and as he moved closer to Seth, who was experiencing a profuse cold sweat with nervousness, he smiled at him, somehow assuaging his angst. "Don't worry, this will help heal you."

He applied the 'medicine', piercing Seth's left arm's skin. Seth began to roar veraciously, then became somnolent and very drowsy, finally falling into a deep sleep.

Lucini grinned with sadistic satisfaction. "What did you give him, Doc?"

"Oh, just something that I've been working on since his arrival. Let me tell you, this young man here is going to make us very rich indeed, and I'm the physician that's going to propel this little dwelling into the limelight."

CHAPTER 5

SETH OPENED his eyes and tried to get himself up out of the hospital bed. Snowdon and Lucini were at their lunch and didn't think to take turns as they were so caught up in how they could exploit him for their own selfish goals. There weren't as many tubes connected to him as in the days earlier. He pulled the drip from his arm, enthralled with a surge of survival, and slowly got up. He heard footsteps coming down the corridor. He gazed around the room and saw the door as his only means of hiding. Lucini opened the door to discover Seth was not lying on his bed where he should have been. Seth pushed the door from the other side into Lucini's face, disorienting him. He then shoved him in a brutal manner to the far corner. Seth put on Lucini's white garment and quickly fled the scene.

On his way down the corridor, he hid in the janitor's room and saw some old, normal clothes. He quickly put them on and headed unnoticed out of Rivers Town General Hospital. He rustled through his pants pockets and found a few twenties; yet again, his instincts were at play. He saw people stepping onto a bus. He mimicked them as coolly as if he had been born here. He paid the driver and sat down in the middle of the bus. Seth began to reminisce about life before he had all this trouble. He thought of the harvest season. There were people working in a market in the village square. They were selling all kinds of fruit, flowers, bread, etc. Horse-driven carriages made their way along the sandy roads. He remembered a young woman called Dina; she was having her face made up by her grandmother. It was hot, and they were seated outdoors.

"Now don't you look pretty!" Dina's grandmother said to her.

"Thanks, Gran. I never thought face paint and lipstick would make me look this good. I sure hope we please Mister Gladstone."

"Since the day you were able to understand, I taught you to pick your partner wisely. Mister Gladstone is a good decider and a fair man."

"You also told me not to put all of my eggs in one basket without compromising my reputation. I did listen, Grandma."

"Ever since you were a little girl, I've instilled in you the importance of picking the right man, and I'm pleased to hear you say that you listened to me."

"How did you know Grandad would be your counterpart?"

"Oh, I knew right away. We clicked, and every fiber in my being told me he was the right man."

Dina's grandmother hugged her granddaughter and smiled. "Now, I have ten hungry farmers to feed. Your fancy man should be here any second now."

Dina smiled, and her grandmother stood up. "Thanks, Grandma!"

Seth's memory of that day turned to the time when a man's voice called out, "Dina! Dina!"

She stood up and turned around to see it was Seth himself who had just called out to her. He was dressed in the era's clothing and carrying a bunch of purple flowers. "You look so beautiful, my love!"

"I could sure use a drink of cold fruit juice right now," Dina said.

Seth went to a nearby table and poured a glass of fruit juice. She drank it down fast, without remorse.

"Thanks, sweetheart. Working on the harvest can make you sweat good. Can I ask you something, Seth?"

"You can ask me anything, my love!"

"From the first moment that you came into my field of vision, I felt it, and then, when I almost drowned in your heavenly blue eyes, I knew you were the right one for me. How did you feel about me the first time you met me, Seth?"

"Exactly the same, Dina, my love."

Dina was gobsmacked by his response. She kissed him. He thought, was this kiss only a dream? Did it really happen? Or was this memory part of just a dream? One thing was certain; now, he realized he was in a nightmare. His love was gone, and with it, the chance of ever seeing her again. Sadness enveloped his soul over the realization that he and Dina never got to complete their partnership and that their truest, natural love would never be consummated. Gladstone had very strict precepts on sex before joining. A prospective couple had to be deemed by law to be compatible first before they could make love. This didn't bother them, as they knew the promise of such pleasure from their mutual expression of love to each other would one day be fulfilled; only in Seth and Dina's case, this wasn't to be.

CHAPTER 6

INSIDE SECTION-S'S main control center, there were four personnel monitoring Moon X. Images of the earth, the moon, and Moon X were displayed on large LCD TV screens. There was a sense of urgency and awe among these young men and women. One man, Mark Northington, seemed perplexed by the findings of his research. "I don't get it! They should collide," he muttered to himself. He began to type mathematical equations, which appeared on his computer screen.

Northington came inside. He was intimidated, to say the least, and all of this pandemonium was a lot to take in even for someone as humble as he.

"If you allow me to introduce Professor Mark Northington. These are Agents Hayes and Agent Kimberly Schmitt," Spence said as he carried out the introductions. "Agent Sanchez should be joining us momentarily."

Kimberly moved over to Northington and gave him a hug followed by a kiss on the cheek. They were old-time colleagues and friends.

"Good to see you again, Kimberly. Congrats on your wedding. You know, of all the work we did, all the investigations, I would have never guessed there was anything like Moon X out there."

"Can you determine anything, Mark?" she asked, confident that he was sure to have a credible answer for her and everyone present.

"My calculations are right, but the projections show the opposite outcome."

Kimberly looked at his data on the screen. "Baffling."

As she spoke those words, the doors opened and in arrived Rick late for the briefing much to the disdain of Secretary Spence. And as Rick made his way to his distant chair, he was greeted with a dirty look from Hayes. "About time, Rick," Hayes muttered toward him. "Everyone, this is Agent Rick Sanchez."

"If I may continue, Moon X and our regular moon are supposed to draw each other into each other's gravitational paths, but projections show they repel each other. That doesn't make sense." Northington said, clearly baffled and trying to get his mind back on track to the issue at hand before Rick's interruption.

"So, maybe you're right, Secretary Spence," replied Northington."

"I couldn't be. That outcome breaks all the laws of physics. It means I have to begin again and do all my calculations from scratch."

Kimberely took a deep breath and said, "Time is not something we've got right now." She began to realize something about his theory. She pondered for a moment and had a realization rushing through her mind. "Just say, hypothetically, something is causing them to break the rules, resulting in the two moons pushing each other away?"

"No, I've been over it a dozen times in my head—it's impossible!" replied Northington.

"What's impossible? Wait! The only way that could cause that scenario is the sudden appearance of Moon X itself. That's it!" she continued.

Northington smiled to himself. "Yes, the sudden appearance of Moon X would cause both gravitational fields' polarity to fluctuate like two magnets with the same sides constantly shifting from positive to negative. That's it, Kimberly. You got it."

"I couldn't have done it without those equations!" replied Kimberly humbly.

Spence grunted, took a sip from his glass of still mineral water and spoke, "All the info and evidence show us that whoever was up there are now probably dead."

"We have to assume some aliens may have fled to Earth -- they could be any number of them anywhere across the world," Hayes urged him.

Northington waved his hand nervously and moved over to Rick and shook his hand. "Good to finally meet you, Rick."

"Can you update me on this critical situation?" Hayes asked Kimberly.

She stood up. "Yes. Moon X is barren. Research has shown it had an atmosphere and was abundant with plant life. Something destroyed all vegetation and whatever intelligent life was on it."

"How 'intelligent' was life on Moon X?" asked Rick quite sardonically.

"They were intelligent enough to make it invisible for who knows how many millennia! Besides the obvious security implications, we now know we're not alone in the universe. They were in our own backyard all along. It is a tragedy that we never got to meet them," replied Kimberly.

"What is the worst that can happen as a result of this new moon in close orbit of our planet?" Spence asked Northington.

Northington cleared his throat. "Since the appearance of Moon X, my team and I have discovered that its gravitational field is charged with the opposite of that of our regular moon."

"So, what does that mean? Are they going to collide with each other?" Spence asked with grave concern.

Northington gave back to him a negative smile and experienced an even more negative realization. "Quite the opposite, in fact -- the two celestial bodies will repel each other."

"That's even better," replied Spence.

"No, it's not. They will each push each other apart from one another so powerfully that the resulting stress will knock each of the two moons out of their respective orbits of the Earth, thus creating unfathomable catastrophes throughout the world," continued Northington.

Spence became increasingly irritated, "Just how in the hell are we meant to stop this?"

Rick turned to Spence, staring straight into his eyes. "We need to get up there and re-cloak Moon X long before that has any chance of happening."

"It will be two years before we're capable of having a ship reach Moon X," Spence replied, irritated and didn't exactly fall in love with the sound of that. "There must be another way. In the meantime, we need to develop a way down here -- some kind of preparations to ensure humanity lives on."

With that said he stood up, got his briefcase, and then left. The others, bearing dismal facial expressions, decided to leave the briefing room too.

CHAPTER 7

AS IN RIVERS TOWN, and all across the world, the heightened state of hysteria and uncertainty were infecting the townsfolk like an epidemic. The town's citizens were boarding up their windows. One citizen looked up at the sky and saw Moon X watching majestically down on him, beckoning him to unravel her enigmatic mystery. At the General Hospital, Dr. Snowdon was staring dismally at the old photograph which featured his missing patient. He massaged his eyes with his fingers. The stress was getting to him. He was about to enter into a state of reverie when he heard a knock on his door. "Come in!" he said.

Lucini arrived inside Snowdon's office. "We have to show this photograph to the FBI. Your patient is definitely from Moon X."

"What? If they find out that we took a certain initiative with him, then we will be locked up and it will all be over!" replied Snowdon. "Damn that Moon X and whatever 'life' is up there!"

"Assuming there is any life still up there. It looks like it's been destroyed."

Snowdon became fearful. "What are you babbling about? Didn't you hear what I just said?"

"Dr. Snowdon -- you have to look at the bigger picture here. We need to tell the authorities. It's probably already over -- over for us all."

"For you, maybe."

"And just what do you mean by that, Doc? If I remember correctly, this was all your doing – your 'certain experiments'."

Snowdon panicked. He was not used to playing the bad guy, even though he had nefarious ambitions throughout his life; putting them into practice was another thing. "You've got to cover me, Lucini. Otherwise, it's toast for both of us."

Lucini grunted to himself and walked out while Snowdon thought fast for a few moments and picked up his cell phone that was lying idle on his desk. An hour later, Lucini met Snowdon yet again, this time to check on Seth. Both men were outside his room. "Still no sign of his return. Just where in the hell is he?" Snowdon asked.

"He could have slipped into the past or future."

"Great! The FBI should've come sooner. Then I wouldn't have given him that concoction of sedatives!"

"It's still not too late yet."

"I consider myself to be a pragmatic man. I guess whatever turmoil is going to happen, will happen."

"Damn it, Snowdon! If you're not going to the FBI, then I will!"

Snowdon shook his head. "If you do, I'll bring you down with me."

With that said Snowdon went into his office to find a strange looking man with his back turned to him. "Who are you and what are you doing in my office?"

This strange looking man turned around and point his finger out toward the window at Moon X. This man was Gladstone. "Puzzling, isn't it? Everybody wondering how it came to be here and just who is up there?"

Snowdon found his voice to be hypnotic. Gladstone's eyes lit up to bright blue and he stared at the corrupt doctor, mesmerizing him. "I want you to help me and my friends out. There's a woman on her way here soon. She's pregnant and it's in my best interests that she bears a strong child especially now. Otherwise, my old friends on this planet will pay the price. Do you understand, Doctor?"

"Yes. But how can you be so sure that she will arrive here? How can you be so certain of that?"

Gladstone smirked. "You see, my friends have gifted me with glimpse of the future. It comes in handy at times. Her name is Sandra."

Gladstone took out a vile from his pocket and handed to Snowdon. "Inject this substance into her blood stream."

Snowdon became fretful. Icy cold shivers ran down his spine like insects crawling speedily. "I'm not a murder! I won't. I'll get into trouble!"

"If you don't do what I ask, then, that's exactly what you will become."

Snowdon took the vile from Gladstone's hand. His hand was shaking and almost dropped it. He knew he was in over his head. "Have you something to do with the young man named Seth?"

"Don't worry about Seth. I know I will be encountering him soon enough."

Gladstone's eyes returned to normal, and he left through the door of Snowdon's office. He went out to find him only there was no sight of him anywhere. It was like if he was never there.

CHAPTER 8

RICK GOT the next plane to New Hampshire and, luckily enough, found Rivers Town. Unbeknownst to him, Sandra was on the same plane as she followed him, following him so she could tell him some important personal news. It had only one hospital, the General Hospital. Nobody knew where he was going. He took a private plane to Rivers Town and, keeping it from Sandra was one thing, but concealing his whereabouts from Hayes was another. As he entered the hospital's sliding doors, he became astonished at how clean and pristine the building was. Rick followed the signs until he came to Snowdon's section. He asked a man who was seated at the reception desk, "Could you let Dr. Snowdon know I'm here?"

"Do I look like a receptionist?" the man answered in an irksome tone. This man was Lucini. This didn't halt Rick in any way, and he pushed further. "He is expecting me. I'm Agent Sanchez."

Lucini knew Rick was not your everyday jerk looking for information on relatives. He picked up the phone. "Excuse me, Doctor. Agent Sanchez is waiting to see you."

"Send him through."

Lucini nodded his head, and Rick got the message, no matter how ignorantly it was conveyed, and went inside. Doctor

Snowdon stood up. He was not a nervous man generally, however, he appeared to be anxious and panicky. He moved closer to Rick. "Thank you for coming, Agent Sanchez. Ordinarily the reason as to why I asked you here would seem to be ludicrous, but, with moons popping out of the sky, you can't leave anything to chance."

"Please, tell me everything. I'm not gonna dismiss you or it."

"Alright. Just one day before that moon appeared... a strange man was found unconscious here in Rivers Town's Main Street. He appeared to be suffering from some kind of radiation poisoning, although the symptoms have me baffled somewhat..."

"Please, Doctor, just the finer details."

Dr. Snowdon began stuttering. He coughed and cleared his throat. "I believe this stranger is from Moon X."

"How?"

"Not 'how,' but when?"

"I'm sorry, you have lost me."

"There is nothing on this planet that could cause such radiation poisoning and still be alive."

Rick laughed and then became more serious. "How?"

"I studied their lesions and they are the result of this radiation poisoning. It could only come from that charcoaled moon – Moon X."

Rick needed a moment to take in what Snowdon was saying. "If this is true, then, what kind of people are capable of achieving this? What the hell is up there?"

Snowdon didn't answer; instead, he laughed grandiosely. "I've been saying the same thing! I think it's a prelude to judgment day!"

Rick sighed with annoyance. "Where is he now?"

Snowdon composed himself and smartened up. "He escaped!"

"Thank you, Dr. Snowdon. That's it for now."

Rick was about to leave the hospital when he saw Sandra

waiting for him inside the door. He was taken aback. "What the hell are you doing here? Do you know I'm on official business?"

"Rick, I'm pregnant and it's yours."

He wasn't having any of this and didn't believe her, and moreover, didn't want to believe her. "You mean you followed me all the way up here to tell me this? I *know* the baby you're carrying is not mine. God knows how many clients you were with before we got married. The father could be anyone!"

She began sobbing and was insulted. "You married me a few weeks ago with all promises that you're a better man now. What happened to that man? How dare you, Rick?! It *is* yours!"

Rick became infuriated. "Sandra, That was before I knew you could be carrying any low life's child. Just go home like I said and leave me to do my work!"

"You haven't changed at all," Sandra said, as she made her way away from him.

Dr. Snowdon overheard the commotion at the door and walked over to Rick and Sandra. "I can't help overhearing your dilemma. I believe that I can be of assistance, Sandra, is it?"

"Yes. Can do a DNA test, right? That will prove that he's the father," she asked the doctor.

"I sure can, dear. Please, both of you come this way. This one's on the house."

Rick became even more embarrassed. "No way! I'm outta here. I've no time to waste on such nonsense."

As Rick cowardly fled the troubling scene, Snowdon reached out to Sandra. She was sobbing and had her right hand placed on her stomach.

"Listen, dear. That offer extends to me doing a full check on your baby."

Sandra wiped the tears from her cheeks and replied, "No, I don't really want to waste your time, doctor."

"It's Dr. Snowdon, and I'm only too happy to help you."

Sandra lay on a bed while Snowdon carried out an ultrasound so he could see the prenatal scans for himself. One of his nurses was present also. After a few moments, as the satisfaction on Snowdon's face turned to horror, he asked politely for the nurse to leave. He turned to Sandra and decided to ask a delicate question to her as gently as he could. "Sandra, I hate asking this, but are you sure Rick Sanchez is the father?"

"Not you too. I'm more than sure!"

"Do you know a man called Seth?"

She didn't answer; instead, she got up from the bed and stormed out of the hospital.

"Wait, I have to ask. There's something else, I believe the child you're carrying has some baffling characteristics."

Sandra became worried. "What?!"

Snowdon thought for a moment. He knew he have to come up with a convincing lie. "I believe you have been exposed to radiation. Ever since that second Moon came here, I find I have to carry out this procedure on all pregnant women in my care. It's just a precaution but I am going to inoculate you."

Sandra didn't like the sound of this. "No! I don't even know you!"

"Do you want your baby to suffer from abnormalities. Look, I can contact your own doctor and fill him in but I'm telling you now in all honesty that if you procrastinate, you're putting your baby at unnecessary risk!" Snowdon urged, rather convincingly.

She paused and momentarily had a reprieve from her angst and found this to be comforting much like the sound of Snowdon's voice. "Okay, do what you have to do."

He took out the same vile that Gladstone had given him earlier and connected it to the syringe. He then injected her. She screamed out loud because the serum hurt like hell as it entered her veins.

"I will now need to do a thorough examination of you," said Snowdon.

As Rick was walking to his car, he heard, "Hey!"

He turned around to find Lucini gesturing for him to come back. "What do *you* want now?"

"Hey, I wouldn't leave your wife alone with that doctor. He gave Seth quite a strange concoction days ago."

"What do you mean 'alone with him'?"

"You'd better find out for yourself."

Rick stormed back into the hospital and into the examination room. As he opened the door, he was greeted by Snowdon telling him to get out, mistakenly thinking he was a nurse. Rick saw Sandra undergoing another pre-foetal scan ultrasound. "Get away from her," he yelled.

"You don't understand. There's something wrong with her pregnancy, Agent Sanchez."

Rick ignored what Snowdon had just said and turned to him angrily. "You're a quack! I'm going to have federal agents swarming all over this hospital investigating you!"

He helped Sandra get up off the bed. "Sandra, will you go home, please, now!"

She carried out his request and, as he watched her put her top back on and leave, he reminisced about the time Rebecca gave him joyful news on the day she told him they were expecting a baby. He remembered how happy they both were and how especially happy she was when she saw how joyous he was when she told him. They planned to buy a house just outside DC so they could give their child the best start and planned to have a large family. Not only did the baby represent their expression of love with Rebecca, but also a positive contribution they were both making to society. Rick saw this child as not only a gift from Rebecca but also from a higher power, and he was determined to do his best in return. On the other hand, with Sandra, his impression was that even if the baby was definitely his, he knew it was off to a shaky start because he was no longer the same man as before, and he didn't view or value Sandra in the same way as his beloved wife.

When Rebecca fell ill with leukaemia, she couldn't carry their baby to term. This was, as Rick perceived, the final straw in which she gave up her fight against the disease. He couldn't watch her being heartbroken any longer and began drinking. First to make it easier to handle everything, then by habit, until it grabbed a hold of him. After her passing, he would drink for days and eventually begin dabbling in women. He decided to quell these painful memories by taking out his hip flask and imbibing from it. Sandra was well gone now, and he was glad that this awkward pain and situation were over, so he hoped.

CHAPTER 9

AS SEEN by millions of people across the world, Moon X was moving closer to our moon. In Washington DC, Rick and Hayes had just finished their coffees at a French bistro. They were on their way to meet with Secretary Spence at the Pentagon. It was now three weeks since the appearance of Moon X. Nobody had any answers as she orbited the earth without permission, which compared to something from a wayward person who came to a family dinner uninvited. They were early, as Spence demanded punctuality at all times. As he perused Section-S's preliminary reports, he found himself becoming disgusted at the lack of real progress. He took a deep breath and decided to hear Rick and Hayes out first before giving them a mouthful. Rick was seated and reluctantly going through reports until Hayes barged in without warning. "Sanchez! Where the hell were you yesterday? I fired your secretary for not telling me! This had better be good."

Rick stood up. "I received a report from a particular Dr Snowdon from some dump called Rivers Town."

"Don't let me hear you belittling anywhere in this fine country of ours."

"Call it what you will. But you should take a look at this."

He handed Hayes his report. Hayes perused it and became impatient. "You expect me to read it all? Give me the gist of it."

"I don't think you're going to like it, or even believe it."

"Just say it, damn it!"

"One human being arrived in Rivers Town. He had unusual radiation lesions. Anyway, I was speaking to Dr Snowdon, and he reckons he came from Moon X."

"Human, did you say?"

"I did, and there's more! He has escaped."

Hayes turned the page and began muttering to himself. Rick continued, "Looks like we're dealing with people who can travel to Earth at will."

The door opened, and in arrived Kimberly and Northington. Hayes immediately turned to Northington. "Mark, tell him your theory," Hayes asked Northington.

Northington cleared his throat. He was a little nervous. "As I told you before, sir, Moon X was spatially and temporally phased from somewhere else into our universe."

"At least give it to me in English!" Rick said.

"Okay. It was 'hiding' outside our space and time."

"How do you even know this?"

Nobody answered him.

Northington interjected, "I have a possible theory as to why this moon has just seemingly appeared," Northington said nervously.

"Go ahead, spit it out!" Spence exhorted.

"It could have been de-cloaked so others could find it. Possibly a rebellion took place on it to prevent this from happening, hence the mass destruction."

"If that's true, then we will need to get to Moon X and re-cloak it before this can happen! Assuming the technology is still usable. Our focal point for surveillance is Rivers Town, New Hampshire. I have people sent there already," Hayes ordered.

CHAPTER 10

ON THE OUTSKIRTS of Rivers Town at the edge of its hamlet-style civilization, Seth Odyssey was gadding about, exploring what seemed to him an alien world. He saw a group of homeless people taking shelter from the rain in a derelict house. Moon X was half-hidden by the clouds, and the homeless people drinking their vodka and beer might as well have been oblivious to its existence. Seth gazed up at the sky. He thought of his beloved Dina. He missed her with a growing, nauseating feeling in his stomach, which intensified with the passing of these long Earth days. He thought of the final hours he was with her as he watched his home. It was in the contradictory futuristic city simply known as Capital City, with its skyline lit up. He and Dina were walking together, along with other couples, on a long path to this mystical town. Dina was exuberant with excitement like a human bride on her wedding day. "The day of our joining is here, my love."

Seth felt the same. This was true love if ever. "I thought I would never see it. Our marriage will be the envy of other couples."

He remembered how Dina extended her right hand toward Seth. He then placed his left hand on hers. "There, we are counterparts in every way."

He also remembered her warm smile as she uttered those

loving words. Seth and Dina entered an insipid room. They were soon instructed by an androgynous-looking individual to become seated on what appeared to be an uncomfortable sofa. Seth seemed nervous and sweated somewhat. This individual he recalled was named Ebenezer. Ebenezer was to be joined with his mate, Eliza, at a ceremony. As Ebenezer entered, he appeared to be in control, displaying a certain tour de force. He had an official position in this society. He made his way along a short corridor where there were four doors on each side. He arrived at the second door on the right. His retina on his left eye was scanned, and the door opened. He was now joined by Eliza.

"I told you that I'd be on time," Ebenezer said softly to her.

"Yes, you did. I should be more trusting of you since we're going to be paired in a few moments," she replied.

"If I ever had a true counterpart to me in every way, I know it is you."

"You're also my true counterpart. I always feared that I'd be a neutral and be forced to live a long, dull life of servitude."

They embraced and kissed. They were soon interrupted by the sound of someone walking down the corridor. It was Madame Official. "Could you two please stop that since you're not paired yet!" she said.

"My apologies, Madame Official," Ebenezer said.

"Administrator Gladstone will see you soon."

Ebenezer and Eliza were joined by two more about the same age. Gladstone was seated at his desk. The first couple were standing beside his desk. They were skinny in build. The second couple were each slightly overweight. Madame Official attached the headpiece on their heads. Their faces didn't display any discomfort. Gladstone checked the readings on the virtual that appeared like a ghostly image beside him. He turned to Ebenezer and Eliza. "Congratulations. You are each a counterpart of one another in all ways that we determine for the correct criteria for a partnership. Go and serve."

Ebenezer and Eliza left the room while the remaining two

couples also got approval from Gladstone. It now was Seth and Dina's turn. They entered Gladstone's office quite humbly. Madame Official placed the headpiece on as Gladstone checked the readings. "I am sorry. Each of you has failed the test to become each other's counterpart. You are not compatible," he snarled. "Not only the fact that she's taller than you, but you both also have similar traits that make you a disaster for a partnership. You are now classified as neutrals. Stay away from each other from this moment on!"

Dina cried as Seth became livid. "Dina and I obeyed all the rules. We love each other, can't you see?!"

"Nevertheless, you two do not meet the correct criteria. Now report to the employment department on your way out. If you can't serve society by providing a family, then you must offer yourselves to work to sustain our planetoid so other families will benefit."

"Wait! We have so much to offer together as a partnership. Dina makes me complete and fills me up with such happiness. This will make us much better workers and more productive members of society!"

"No! I decide which individuals join with each other in a couple. The tests say you both are not compatible. I can't allow ancient emotional attachments to dictate partnerships. Go and find someone else and come again, or else you will be arrested."

Dina pulled out a long needle from her jacket and tried to stab Gladstone. She failed dismally, and the needle dropped to the ground. Security saw what just happened and fired at her. She pushed herself in front of them and got the impact of the bullet. Seth screamed and rushed over to her to check if she was still alive. Her blood was everywhere, and she struggled to speak. Seth was distraught and in disbelief. "Dina, baby. Don't leave me! I love you! I need you!"

"I love you, Seth. If we can't be together here, maybe we can in the hereafter."

She closed her eyes and passed away. Seth roared with voracious anger. The security cuffed him and took him into custody. As the security were escorting him away, Gladstone began to preach. "Neutrals never make counterparts! Too much in common is intrinsically flawed. Arrest him!"

Seth was restrained by the guards and taken away.

CHAPTER 11

AS PEOPLE across the world stared up at the tri-light sky, they realized the end of life was a very frightening, perplexing possibility. Seth and his newfound friends couldn't really care less, though. For them, their lives had ceased a long time ago. He saw four homeless people begging off passersby. Other homeless people were lying around outside an abandoned building on the fringes of Rivers Town. He walked around this building, exhausted. His luck to a certain degree was about to change, however, when he spotted a man with a six-pack of beer. Seth approached this man without a sense of bravery but more out of desperation. "Excuse me, Sir. Could I imbibe?"

The man just gave him a filthy look. Seth asked again.

"Get your own!" the man replied.

Another homeless man, who happened to notice Seth was in distress, approached. His name was Tim. "Here, fellow, have some of mine," Tim said as he handed Seth a bottle of whisky. "I think that new moon is making everybody thirsty, eh?"

Seth looked up to the sky and frowned.

"Hey, fellow, is it just me seeing two moons, or is it really there?" Tim continued.

"Believe me, it's there. Thanks for the flavoured water."

"It's called 'whisky,' man! Where have you been?"

Seth moved away slowly.

"Hey, man! Where are you going already? You haven't heard my troubles yet! I got more booze. Some poor idiot died and left me twenty bucks."

Seth turned around and took another drink.

"That's more like it, man. My name is Tim. What's yours?"

"Seth."

"Well, Seth, the aliens will soon be arriving to enslave us all!"

"No. Not now."

"Whatever. Tell me, Seth, do you have a wife, girlfriend, or both?"

Seth didn't reply.

"I, myself, don't have much luck with the ladies. It's a shame, man, 'cos I have great ambitions to be with them," Tim said.

"I'm sorry for you."

"Don't be sorry, man. Tell me, what's your name again?"

"Seth."

"Yeah, Seth. They don't find me congenial."

"You were seen as incompatible with your potential mates?"

"Incompatible? Since when has anybody ever been compatible?"

"My friend, this society has denied you as well as me."

"How so?"

"I was robbed of my joining, all because my world was influenced and based on this elitist society."

"Tell me about it. It seems if you're not hot, you don't get to be successful with women, men, or both if that's your fancy. I mean, the right look with the right body opens up doors…"

"Your world is sick. You're wrong. You seem congenial to people to me."

"Don't get me wrong. I was a player until I got this disease."

Tim pointed to the bottle.

Seth was not finished speaking. "A society where most want to live to excess."

"You sound weird. Just where the hell are you from, Seth?"

"I come from up there," Seth replied, pointing to Moon X.

Tim didn't believe him. "Man, my whisky sure went to your brain. Say, could you lend me twenty bucks?"

Seth shook his head. "I'll put this right for all of us!"

He then walked off, stopped, and gazed up at his once home, recalling his last time on Moon X and the fateful hour he sold his soul. These were the last few moments when he entered the room that controlled the Stealth Mechanism. He was wearing a gas mask, and to his surprise, Gladstone was not even present, only his scientists and technicians. Gladstone toured this facility regularly on a daily basis, but as irony would have it, not on this day.

Seth had with him a small container, and before the scientists could utter a question as to what he was doing there, he pulled off the container's lid. A golden gaseous cloud billowed from the container and soon filled the room. The people there choked to death within seconds. Some of them struggled to approach him but quickly died. Seth threw the container on the ground and rushed over to the main computer console, where he began working on it frantically. He experienced a profuse cold sweat and muttered to himself, "Got you now, Gladstone!"

Gladstone was blissfully unaware of the transpirations in the Stealth Mechanism control center. He was studying virtual images of the human brain. "Madame Official!"

Madame Official entered his office. "Any luck?"

Gladstone smiled. "Yes, indeed. The last couples I made counterparts are matching the schematics."

"Finally."

"The Benefactors will be most pleased."

Suddenly, the strident sound of an alarm could be heard. Gladstone stood up. "It's the alarm for this building, which means there has been a security breach."

He moved over to his observation monitor. Images of his building and the surrounding Capital City appeared on the screen. He quickly, carefully watched his building's layout.

"The stealth creating system!" He ran out of his office and headed down an empty corridor.

Seth was finished at the console he was working on. He then moved over to the far end of this room. There was what appeared to be a chamber located inside an alcove. A retina scanning device reached out to his face and scanned his right eye, followed by an electronic voice saying, "Access denied!"

He sighed and instinctively allowed the device to scan his left eye.

"Access granted!" the electronic voice sounded.

The alcove's doors opened. Seth stepped inside and closed the doors behind him.

"Computer, remove Stealth Phasing Shield!" he said.

"Affirmative! Stealth shielding will collapse in less than twenty minutes."

The planet Earth and her singular moon appeared contractively tranquil. Seth stepped out from the alcove. The entrance of this room opened, and as he was fully out of the alcove, Gladstone was waiting there for him, holding a dagger. Seth began to panic. Gladstone could perceive his fear emanating from him and yelled, "Seth Odyssey! How did you acquire special knowledge to breach security?"

A humble, nervous Seth responded, "This is my revenge!"

"Why the hell did you do that?" Gladstone angrily asked. He then rushed over to the alcove and quickly discovered he couldn't access it. Seth began to push random buttons on each console. Gladstone fired a shot at him from a rifle he just picked up from the ground and missed. Seth managed to leave the room unharmed. A much louder electronic voice broadcasted all over Capital City, "Warning alert! Subatomic radiation has reached toxic levels and will burn out all biological life and vegetation on this planetoid within minutes!"

Shock and awe consumed Gladstone. He pondered for a moment. "Computer, prepare to evacuate!"

"Negative action -- insufficient time remaining."

"What have you done, Seth Odyssey?" He cried as he ran out of the vicinity to his office where Madame Official was waiting. "We have to get out of here right now!" he exhorted.

Madame Official didn't respond to him and remained motionless.

"Don't you understand, woman?"

"I do not belong down there, and neither do you. It would be a violation!"

Gladstone turned around and sighed with deepening frustration. As his back was facing her, she pulled out his dagger from his holster and tried to stab him. He moved to the left-hand side of her and became startled, dropping the weapon. She managed to kick him in the stomach, winding him, only he was much stronger than her. She was about to pick up the dagger, but he kicked it away in time. He got himself upright and pounced on her, almost flattening her with his stomach. He grabbed the dagger and stabbed the life out of her. An eternal moment passed by. He rushed over to his desk. "Computer, initiate emergency personal escape shuttle."

The electronic voice responded, "Launch will take place in less than four minutes!"

Suddenly, about three-quarters of the distance between the moon and the earth, there was an eruption in space. Within seconds, a second moon emerged from this distortion, followed by two small shuttles departing from this second moon, which became notoriously called Moon X.

Seth stopped reminiscing, and a surge of feelings of guilt pumped through his veins. He felt violently sick with the swirling anxiety growing ever potently from his stomach to his brain. It was only when a car pulled up beside him and Tim that he was granted a reprieve from those very unpleasant emotions. "Seth? Seth, is that you?"

Seth began to panic but was much too inebriated to run away from the car. The driver gathered speed and pursued him vehemently until Seth backed him into a narrow corner. He could hear the car doors opening, and he reluctantly turned around to face the driver, and to his unpleasant surprise, discovered it was indeed Dr. Snowdon who was behind the wheel. Snowdon got out and implored, "Seth, please allow me to help you! I need to help you!"

"You will only lock me up again!"

"Seth!"

"Noooh!" Seth yelled as he ran off.

Snowdon chased him and managed to calm him down. "Seth, they're all searching for you! Look, I can offer you protection! Please, allow me to do that for you?"

"Can you keep me safe from the authorities?"

"I sure can," Snowdon replied, smiling.

Seth followed Snowdon to his car, got in, and they drove back to Rivers Town. As Snowdon stopped at a gas station to buy petrol, he didn't see Nadia cycling nearby. She caught a glimpse of Seth in the driver's seat. She went over to ask if he was okay when Snowdon came over to his car to fill the tank up. He hissed at her to get away. "Seth? Seth? You're special!" Nadia yelled and then realized immediately to whom Snowdon was. Rivers Town was a small town, and everybody knew everybody else and their personal business. She headed off home contemplating that this Seth had something to do with Moon X. she had broken up with James as he grew sick of her obsession with everything to do with the extra moon watching like a vengeful instrument of divine retribution over the world. He kicked her out of his apartment two weeks ago and his final words to her were, "You're wired to that thing in the sky."

When they got back there, Snowdon had planned a little surprise for Seth. As he showed him the hospital basement where he said he would be safe from the authorities, he stabbed him in the arm with a syringe full of tranquillisers. He tied him to a chair, strapping him to it with duct tape. When he awoke, he tried to move and talk. Even though his mouth was not covered, he still struggled to speak, mainly due to the long-lasting effect of the tranquillisers. Snowdon took out another syringe. This time it was a much stronger dosage of the same drugs. "My most humble apologies, Seth. I'm afraid I can't risk you escaping again. Agent Sanchez will be here soon. It will be all over for both of us then."

CHAPTER 12

EARLY MORNING TIME in Rivers Town was characterised by Moon X being dominantly vivid in the cloudy sky. People went about their business now without giving her a second thought, except for Snowdon, who became more preoccupied by her every passing moment. Rick's car pulled up outside the hospital. He got out, slamming the door behind him. He made his way to the entrance until he was interrupted by Nadia. "Detective! Detective, are you looking for Seth?"

"How do you know about him, dear?" asked Rick.

"I was one of the people who first found him. I saw him in Dr. Snowdon's car yesterday. God only knows what they're doing to him."

"You go home, darling. I'll hand it from here."

Rick placed his arm on Nadia's shoulder to comfort her and headed inside the hospital. As he was walking toward the building, Nadia pleaded with him to take care of Seth.

Now inside, Rick looked around and didn't recognize anybody. Lucini happened to come out of the bathroom. Rick quickly approached him. "You! The receptionist!"

"You again."

"I know Seth is here in this building!"

Lucini became reluctant to cooperate with Rick. Rick caught

him and pushed him up against the wall raising him up from the ground. Lucini had met his match and knew it. "Okay, okay. The Doc told me he made a deal with the FBI. Should he find that freak, then they would drop his investigation."

"Take me to Snowdon now!"

"I haven't seen him since yesterday morning. He has Seth! I have to point out that he's been acting strangely lately."

They both searched every ward until it struck Lucini that the basement was one possible place he could be. They made their way by the elevator to that location. When they got there, they were both astounded at what they saw. "What have you done?" Lucini yelled.

Snowdon didn't answer; he was unable to answer. Rick moved over to Seth to find him unconscious. "What the hell's the matter with Snowdon?"

"He's dead," replied Seth. "He carried out torture on me as if I hadn't been through enough of that already."

Lucini moved over closer to check out Snowdon's corpse. "Dumb bastard. He thought he knew everything. I did tell him."

"Enough?! There's nothing we can do for him now, but I need your help in getting Seth to my car," Rick said urgently.

Later on, back in Washington, DC, and far from the proper proceedings that we all hoped took place in the confines of the Pentagon, there was something not proper taking place in an old warehouse just outside the suburbs of DC. Rick had Seth tied to a chair that was reminiscent of the late Snowdon's forced imprisonment of him. Instead of duct tape, he was handcuffed, and his legs were chained to a steel chair. The room was half-lit and dusty but dry, as opposed to the dampness of the Rivers Town hospital's basement that unsettled Seth a little.

The loud, noisy door could be heard opening that shrieked Seth's nerves even more as someone else was coming inside the warehouse. Seth flinched as he saw a stocky, tough figure of a man that was Hayes coming over to scrutinize him. They heard rain beginning to belt down on the roof. The dryness of the room becoming ever so damp. Seth began to believe his time of reckoning was here and he would be punished for what he thought now were his unforgivable crimes. He wanted a way to redeem himself.

Hayes was feeling uncomfortable with this situation, while Rick was determined to finally have answers. Hayes turned to Rick and whispered, "He's not gonna talk. Just look at him. I've dealt with all kinds of scum, I mean the lowest of the low, and some psychos even the insane would give a dead smile, but this guy must have his brains fried from all that radiation..."

Rick placed his hand on Hayes's shoulder. "Let me try."

Rick moved closer to Seth and circled him. He then smiled at his prisoner with a friendly expression. "Hello, Seth. It can't be too comfortable being held together by the restraints. Allow me..." he said warmly. He then took out a bunch of small keys from his pocket and unlocked Seth's handcuffs. Seth stretched himself and placed his hands on his knees.

"That's much better, isn't it?" he continued.

Seth nodded his head and uttered, "Fielding never counted on me falling in love! I was meant to make sure Gladstone was kept in line."

Rick and Hayes's attention was piqued. "Who's 'Fielding'?" Rick asked. Seth laughed aloud. "Never mind, Fielding. Gladstone's gonna get you!" replied Seth, laughing hideously.

Hayes quickly lost his temper and approached Seth. He then slapped him across the face. "We've had enough of this horseshit! Just who the hell are you and why are you here?"

Rick hurriedly went over to Hayes and pulled him away from Seth. "What the hell are you doing, Hayes? For God's sake, compose yourself! He's all we got!"

"He'd better give us clear explanations soon, or I'll beat the crap out of you too, as well as him!"

"I'm getting there... Just shut up!"

Rick turned yet again to Seth. "My apologies for my boss, but, Seth, you must give us answers."

"I'm from up there -- that new moon, and I killed everybody on it. I didn't mean to. I did it because Gladstone murdered Dina, my counterpart."

"Was Dina going to be your wife?"

"Yes."

"That sucks, Seth. That really does. I know what it feels like to have your one true love grabbed from you, and all you can do is stand idly by and watch. In my case, it was my wife, Rebecca. She got sick. After that, all I did were self-destructive things that made my life even more painful."

Seth wept, "That pain is so intense that it clouds your judgement, making you do evil acts."

Rick nodded in agreement. After all, he knew what this young man was saying to be true, and he couldn't deny it. Then he realized he was slightly harsh with Sandra and needed to fix it. He turned to Seth and posited his mind back on his job, to be more specific, the matter at hand. "Has this something to do with that guy, what did you say his name was?"

"Fielding?"

"Yeah, Fielding."

"Fielding implanted markers in my DNA to enable me to perceive his memories. If Gladstone gets to the Benefactors before you, then he will succeed."

"Just who the hell are the 'Benefactors'?" Hayes asked.

"I don't know any more."

"How can we get to Gladstone and re-cloak Moon X?" Rick continued.

"I have a spacecraft."

Rick turned to Hayes and they both smiled. "Where? How?"

"It's located just outside Rivers Town, and it's cloaked like my home was.

BOTH MOONS COULD BE SEEN with an eerie, menacing harmony in the North Eastern night sky over Rivers Town. A convoy of FBI jeeps followed by Hayes's transport consisting of escorted cars by the Police paraded through the outskirts of this now pivotal hamlet. Hayes's jeep pulled up and he and Rick got out. Kimberly and Northington followed them. A second jeep pulled up beside Hayes's and three armed soldiers escorted out Seth. Hayes was adamant that things were going to go his way. He grabbed Rick's arm, "Keep a close eye on Seth. He's a crafty bastard and I don't want any screw-ups!"

"Where's his ship?" asked Rick with a morbid sense of curiosity.

"Didn't you hear what I just said?!"

"Sure. I won't let him piss sideways."

Hayes sighed with worry. He doubted Rick because he was too clean-cut and all of a sudden was trying to be a hard guy. The soldiers brought Seth over to them. Kimberly and Northington joined them. Hayes nudged Seth slightly, "So where is it?"

"Not far," replied Seth.

He pointed to an area just a couple hundred meters away. It was what appeared to be an empty field. "Just over here..."

Northington moved closer to him. "Mister Odyssey, my

name's Mark. I would really like it if we could discuss in more detail how all this works. I'd --,"

"Shut up, Northington!" Rick yelled at him.

"Don't tell him to shut up!" Kimberly yelled back at him.

"Enough!" Hayes welcomingly interjected.

They arrived at the outskirts of the field. Seth began to whistle a mellifluous tone. The empty area of the field began to quiver, which was followed by a distortion in mid-air. Seth's shuttlecraft soon emerged from nothing and became fully visible to everybody.

"Nice going!" Kimberly said in awe.

Northington smiled at Kimberly and then to everyone else.

Hayes was taken aback. "Right, Seth. You said this craft is big enough to hold four people, including you; how convenient?"

"Yes."

"I want you, Rick, and two equipped personnel to join you..."

Kimberly didn't like the sound of this. "Wait a second here, sir!"

"Yes, Kimberly?" Hayes replied.

"I was under the impression the four of us were coming?"

"The ship only fits four. He could try anything."

"Sir, she's right. It should be myself, her, and even Northington who join Seth," Rick said.

"Rick, are you nuts?" replied Hayes.

"No. It makes perfect sense. Our first contact with the Benefactors shouldn't be hostile."

Hayes was still unsure. "I don't know." He then turned to Seth. "Can you still fly this thing?"

"My shuttle pod can withstand most forces of nature, and yes, I am very capable still."

"Right! I want the three of you to join ET here... get to that moon and do whatever it takes to preserve humanity!" Hayes yelled.

Suddenly they heard the bushes rustling and Sandra came out of nowhere.

"Who is this woman?" Hayes asked.

Sandra went over to Rick and slapped him across the face. "I followed you all here and just who is this Seth?"

Hayes turned to Rick. "How does she know his name, Sanchez?"

"I don't know," he replied, shocked at what she just asked him.

"She must know," continued Hayes.

Sandra became almost hysterical and began yelling. "All I know is that I'm pregnant and there's something strange going on with the very child I'm carrying. Snowdon carried out a very detailed ultrasound and discovered something probably related to Moon X!"

"This is all preposterous!" Hayes exclaimed. "Next she'll ask for a seat to that goddamn moon."

"She can have mine," Kimberly told Hayes.

"Are you serious?" he asked her.

Kimberly smiled at Sandra and this smile was reciprocated. "This woman's life is at risk. The answers are up there on that moon. I started working at Section-S to save lives. I will monitor things down here.

"This is just great," said Rick, clearly pissed off at this ever-dynamic situation.

Seth guided Sandra, Northington, and Rick inside his Shuttle Pod. Over the night sky of Rivers Town, Seth's shuttle could be seen taking off and leaving the town. It then disappeared when it re-cloaked. As the craft entered and left the upper atmosphere of the Earth, the passengers could witness the moon and Moon X in cosmic majesty. Moments later, Seth's shuttle de-cloaked and was now visible set against this celestial quandary.

Inside the craft, it was cramped with Seth piloting and Rick beside him. Sandra and Northington were seated behind them. Northington was watching everything with astonishment akin to childlike wonder. "I can't believe we're in outer space! Look! The moon and the other...,"

"You can say it. My precious home which I destroyed," Seth replied.

Northington was trying to find the right thing to say, "Well... I'm sure you had your reasons... I guess..."

"Right, Seth. Take us to your home," Rick ordered.

Seth worked on his control console. The shuttle swerved and veered toward Moon X.

The celestial body that was Moon X appeared barren, as if a massive deluge of fire had ravaged the planetoid's vegetation and plant life. There were hundreds of skeletons scattered all over. The glorious Earth could be seen in the sky, as our distant moon, orbiting it. Seth's shuttle landed on what appeared to be a metallic docking pad.

The craft's hatch opened up, and the crew, led by Rick, slowly and cautiously exited it. Rick and his crew were in awe at what they were experiencing, while Seth was nonchalant. This place was his home, and it was nothing new to him. He pointed to the silhouette on the horizon of the dishevelled Capital City, which was now just ruins.

Sandra and Northington were so in shock and awe that they were virtually unable to speak to each other. She picked up a dead flower and showed it to Northington. He smiled but then was saddened by what the dead flower represented. There were also two skeletons nearby. "This place must have been so beautiful," she said. "Those poor people!"

"You can count on mankind to destroy a paradise," Northington replied.

Just then, they looked at the flower again, and it appeared to be healthy, as if it had just been pulled from its roots.

"How could this be? Only moments ago it was dead," she asked Northington.

"This is one sure strange place."

They went over to where Rick and Seth were. Sandra showed her husband the flower, and they gazed toward the horizon and were stunned at what they saw. The polygonal buildings were also regenerating themselves to their original structures. This infuriated Seth, "No! We can't let that happen!"

"Why not, Seth?" Rick asked him.

"This planetoid has a self-restoring capability. It can restore itself back to what it was before I destroyed it! Fielding's genetic markers in my DNA are telling me the Benefactors will now be able to find it!"

"And if the Benefactors find Moon X, Earth is at risk. Can the population you killed be restored also?"

"No."

"Can we trust this guy?" Sandra asked her husband.

"What choice have we got?" he replied. "How do we prevent this from happening?" he asked Seth.

"We must get to the control matrix as soon as possible and switch this process off for good."

"Take us there now!"

Seth led the way to the now self-restoring capital city. As he was walking, he experienced a vertiginous state. Everything became distorted around him, and a figure of a person came out of this mist-like distorting clouds. As this person moved closer to Seth, his identity became known as Fielding. "Fielding?" a bewildered Seth asked.

"Yes, Seth. It's me," Fielding replied.

"Can the others see you?"

"No, I'm afraid not. The genetic markers I inserted in your DNA when you were just a clone make it possible for only you to see me. At first, you experienced me as a separate consciousness alongside your own. Now, I'm here with you, fully interactive with all my knowledge."

"I murdered countless thousands. There must be a way I can make amends?"

"Prevent the Benefactors from harvesting humanity. That's the only true way you can redeem yourself."

"I will do my best, even at the cost of my own life. I want you to know I'm truly sorry."

"What's your next move?"

"I have made friends from Earth, and they're here to assist me. We're going to the control matrix."

"That's good. When you're there, summon me by your instinct, and I'll guide you on how to shut it down. In the meantime, be careful."

"Wait!" Seth said to Fielding as he was about to turn his back and walk off. "Was she real? Dina? Did I really know her, and did the time and kiss with her ever really take place?

"Seth, my boy. Most of it was, and let me tell you something: the love you both experienced for each other was real. You both felt it, and that's what makes it real and worthwhile. I'm sorry that you two could never be fully together in the way it mattered."

Fielding vanished, and Seth reverted back to normal.

"Seth, what happened?" Rick asked him.

"Fielding, he has just revealed himself to me. He can guide us in ways I thought weren't possible."

"What kind of ways, Seth?"

"Like an interactive computer program."

"Wow!" Northington said.

"Just how far away is that city?" Sandra asked Seth.

"We should be there in about half one of your Earth days."

CHAPTER 14

THE OUTSKIRTS of the Capitol City were barren, devoid of the self-restoration that was taking place inside this futuristic town. The polygonal glass structures had nearly finished being fully restored. Rick, Sandra, Seth, and Northington had arrived at the city's entrance to discover that there was a long path leading into the center where the Capitol was located, and more importantly, the control matrix. "It won't take long for us to reach the Administrator's building. That's where the control matrix is located," Seth said confidently to the others.

"Let's get going!" Rick replied.

They headed off down the path, staring at these alien structures with wonder and fear. An hour later, they were outside the Capitol. "We must hurry!" Seth urged.

"I sure hope you know what you're doing, Seth," Rick implored.

"Fielding will show me."

They went inside and arrived at Gladstone's office to find it vacant. "Was this Gladstone's office?" Rick asked Seth.

"Yes. Come on -- we don't have much time."

They quickly left Gladstone's office. It gave them all the creeps, and they went into the Main Control Center. The equipment was all fried and melded together. "Oh, no. It's ruined!" Seth screamed.

"What do you mean?" Rick asked.

"The control matrix is fried. We'll never repair it in time. I don't think it's even possible to repair it!"

Suddenly, they heard footsteps moving steadily toward the vicinity. Northington was startled. "Who's that?"

A loud voice exclaimed, "Welcome back, Seth! You traitor!"

"It's Gladstone -- get out of here now!" Seth yelled.

Rick and Sandra converged closer to each other while Northington went out the wrong way, only to be caught by one of Gladstone's guards. Gladstone entered the room. "Get back here, all of you, or he gets it!"

They all did as they were told. Gladstone shoved Northington into the others, and the guards surrounded them all. Gladstone looked at them, and in particular at Seth. "Seth, you Judas! How I'm going to make you suffer to pay for all the inconvenience you've caused me, not to mention almost one million people that you murdered in cold blood."

"You should've let me and Dina become counterparts! This is on you too!"

"Oh, don't be silly. You two were simply inferior in every way and to each other, and now I'm forced to bring the Benefactors here to harvest the Earth for suitable specimens, or maybe I should look closer to home."

He moved over to Sandra, then to Rick, and finally to Northington. "Which of these fine, strapping young men tickle your fancy?" he asked Sandra.

"What?!" Sandra said, shocked.

Rick pushed Gladstone. "Leave her alone!"

"That's good. He's very protective of you, my dear. However, you're going to have to mate with the other one too."

"Screw you, Gladstone!" Rick yelled.

"Guards, get them ready. I want her and those two men tested right away."

The guards escorted Rick, Sandra, and Northington off while Seth remained. "What are you going to do with me?"

"Now that's a pickle, Seth. How do I punish the disloyal subject who murdered my kingdom? I'm going to have to think long and hard about that," he replied and then ordered his guards, "Throw him in a cell for now. I'll deal with him when I think of something."

Sandra was being held in a medical examination room deep inside the halls of the Capitol. She was held down by restraints and was screaming for her husband. Moments later, a new cloned copy of Madame Official stepped inside with a large needled syringe and injected Sandra until she passed out. Meanwhile, Gladstone was in his office, seated at his desk. He was using a virtual display featuring a schematic of the now self-restoring capital city. Madame Official coming inside interrupted him. "She's with child."

"I know. I have already had a doctor down on Earth administer the first dosage of the serum."

"Excellent," replied Madame Official. "That should expediate matters. How much longer will it take for them to arrive?" she asked, somewhat worried.

"They have launched a probe. It should find us in two days or less."

Rick and Northington were being kept against their will not far away from Sandra's location. They appeared to be comfortable and were patrolled by two guards at the entrance that was contained by an energy field. Seconds later, Gladstone arrived outside the entrance of the cell. He gestured grandiosely to the guards to reduce the energy field. Rick quickly rushed over to his side of the opening. "If you have hurt her, I swear I'll make you suffer, Gladstone."

"Sandra is pregnant. However, I wouldn't go celebrating just yet, especially since I got plans for your offspring. All of your offspring!"

"Just what do you mean by that?"

"I mean Sandra is going to mate with you again and again and repeatedly with Northington here until the Benefactors are satisfied. Otherwise, they will harvest that shiny blue planet of yours."

Northington was reviled just as much as Rick. "I will never agree to this!"

Gladstone laughed and with a tone of pompousness replied, "Any acts of refusal to my orders will result in very painful punishments for Sandra."

Seth was lying supine on a bed. He was awake and in deep contemplation about what nefarious plans Gladstone had for him and his friends. His reverie was interrupted when he heard someone in his cell. He got up and saw Fielding as if he was really there in the flesh, free from distorting visual effects like before.

"Fielding?"

"Yes, it's me, Seth."

"How can I get out of this holding cell?"

"Think, Seth. The knowledge is within you."

Seth moved over to the control pad on the wall. There were numbered buttons on it. He concentrated hard and typed a code as if from memory. The force field vanished.

"Good, Seth. Now do the same for your friends."

"How did you know I had friends locked up too?"

"Remember, my memories are joined with yours."

Seth quickly left his cell and managed to sneak over to Rick and Northington's cell where they were silent, waiting in vain for a miracle. Suddenly the force field was gone and they heard Seth whispering, "Come on!"

They immediately followed him out of the cell.

He guided Rick and Northington out of the prison. Two guards saw them. They ran.

"Stop there!" the guards demanded.

They continued running. One of the guards discharged his weapon. Northington got hit on the left leg. He fell. Rick helped him up and linked arms with him. They managed to get outside from the building's right-hand side. Seth pulled the door shut.

"We have to find Sandra!" Rick demanded.

"I can help you but first we need your friend to get back on his feet," Seth replied.

"I'll be okay," Northington said humbly.

"You're hurt badly," Rick urged him.

"Just listen to Seth, Rick!"

A police tram pulled up. They hid beside the prison building and as the officers got out of the tram, Seth whistled. The officers' attention was drawn to the side of the building. They saw Northington wounded, then Seth and Rick from behind jumped onto their backs with full force. Seth grabbed one of their weapons and fired on the two of them, killing them. He then gestured to Rick to help Northington into the back of the tram. Rick kept a lookout as he helped Seth. They made it and Seth powered up the tram and drove off. Northington lay across the back two seats. Rick was in front with Seth driving. Rick turned to Seth, "Do you know where they are keeping Sandra?"

"They probably have brought her to the medical center by now."

"We need to go there right now!"

"Look, Gladstone may have believed I was stupid but don't you! We need to be prepared! I know where I can get weapons."

"Fine. You're right."

Rick turned to Northington and asked, "How are you back there?"

"He's right. We can't take on an army."

"You said you murdered everybody here but how come Gladstone and his private police force are still alive?" Rick asked Seth.

"Because they're super clones!"

"What do you mean?"

"They're all enhanced genetically. It will be very difficult to defeat him."

CHAPTER 15

RICK, Northington, and Seth were now in the wilderness that was once productive farmland. They arrived at an old wheat-farming house that was constructed of metal alloys and was small and rectangular-shaped. All the houses on Moon X, including the polygonal-shaped buildings in Capital City, were designed with optimal efficiency in mind. These plentiful farmhouses were scattered across the planetoid.

They got out of the jeep and carried Northington inside. Rick was astounded by the building's sheer simplicity and asked Seth, "Is this your home?"

"No. It's my uncle's. At least, whom I thought was my uncle. Gladstone duped us clones into thinking we had parents and siblings. It was all a lie."

"Still, you must regret doing what you did?"

Seth didn't answer him.

The interior of Seth's uncle's house was clean and simple, much like homes on Earth. Rick placed his right hand on Northington's left shoulder and said, "Hang in there, Mark. This will all be over soon."

"Help me get him to the basement," Seth urged and then opened a trap door using a remote control pad that he just found hidden under the window.

Both he and Rick carried Northington down the basement stairway.

Scattered in piles across the basement were weapons similar to those used by Gladstone's police force. Rick immediately saw the opportunity here. "Where did you get these?"

"My uncle worked in the official police with Fielding. I can't believe he had all this ammunition."

"It's like he was expecting you to need them someday. There's enough here to take out a small army!" Rick said, astounded.

"That's precisely not what we're going to do. Gladstone will know we're here. We have to set a trap."

"Let's get started."

A short time later, an array of booby traps had been set up. Seth pushed a button on the remote control and it became cloaked. "That should teach them. There is another basement and I'm pretty sure Gladstone doesn't know about it. Here, help me."

Rick moved closer to Seth and pulled up a hatch to reveal another stairway. "It's going to be difficult carrying Northington down these stairs."

Suddenly, they both heard Northington roar followed by Gladstone's police entering the farmhouse.

"They're here! Come on!" Seth urged.

Rick went first and Seth followed down the old stairway. As the police guards came down to the first basement, Seth pushed another button on the remote control. The farmhouse exploded with a strident bang. There was dust and dirt falling on top of Gladstone's police, killing them. Rick paused for a moment and then continued down the stairway. They arrived deeper underground and Seth pulled another hatch open. They jumped into a second, older basement. This was dirty; however, there were guns and rifles stacked up in the corners. Seth went over to the far right corner and picked up a rifle. He checked its settings. "I can't believe it -- it's almost fully charged!"

"Poor Northington. They killed him. We've wasted enough time already. Sandra's in dire danger."

"These two rifles are the best and fully charged."

Rick and Seth were now back outside witnessing the destruction and saw the dead bodies of the police. Without giving it a second thought, they pulled off in the tram cart for the Medical Center. Inside the Medical Center, Sandra was seated and feeling dispassionate. Madame Official accompanied her. "You're not taking my baby!"

Madame Official didn't respond, only simpered a broken smile of contempt toward Sandra. A moment later, the doors opened and in arrived Gladstone. He moved closer to Sandra. "How is our expectant mother keeping now?" he asked.

"It's only a matter of time before Rick Sanchez kicks your ass!"

"We'll have to do something about that foul mouth of yours. I never allowed anybody to speak to me like that when I had a kingdom to rule but thanks to Seth Odyssey, he took that from me. I suppose your litter will be the beginning of a new kingdom -- one that I'll make sure nobody ever conquers again."

"Screw you, Gladstone!"

"Sandra, don't allow your fear of the future to jeopardize the present... it's better this way. Just think of the millions of lives you will be saving on dear old Earth."

"You seem to be vehemently opposed to harvesting the Earth, why?"

"Because your planet is full of the most wayward humans possible. I am a child of your world. That's right! I was born on your Earth. Only for a very wise but stupid man called Fielding, brought me to this planetoid and then I guess I became infected with the specter of the lust for absolute power. The people I grew up with are certainly not good enough for the Benefactors and never will be."

"Next you'll tell me that I should feel honoured that you've chosen me."

"Yes, indeed you should feel honoured and I more than chose you. You see I have a powerful gift of precognition. I knew it was you all along because I knew Fielding had interfered with the night you and your husband conceived your child which made it easy for me to track you down. Remember a Doctor Snowdon? I had him first inject you with a serum to increase your baby's vitality," he replied, turning to Madame Official, "Are you ready to begin the preliminary tests?"

"No!" cried Sandra.

Madame Official nodded and moved over to a compartment and took out a large syringe. Sandra screamed. Madame Official was interrupted by the sound of weapons fire and dropped the syringe.

"I told you he'd come!" Sandra yelled.

"Guards, get them now!" Gladstone yelled.

Seth and Rick fired their particle rifles at Gladstone's guards in the Medical Center's corridors. Seth threw a grenade at a door. There was an explosion. As the smoke billowed, both Seth and Rick waited a moment, and then they entered Sandra's holding room. Rick saw her and charged toward her with unyielding force and passion. Gladstone was gone. Seth fired at Madame Official and killed her.

"Sandra, are you alright?" Rick asked lovingly to his wife.

"You got here just in time before they were about to inject me with something."

"Seth, help me get her back on her feet!"

Seth rushed to them and helped him. They both lifted Sandra gently onto her feet.

"We've got to get out of here fast, Gladstone will be back with reinforcements," Seth said.

"That's right, Seth. Always predictable," Gladstone said as one slightly injured guard came back inside the room.

Rick moved closer to Sandra, while Seth reluctantly joined them. "There's no way, Gladstone that I'm letting you use her as some kind of mass breeder!" Rick said.

"I should offer my congratulations as you are the child's father. I certainly hope that I don't have to use Plan B. Despite my tenacity to my work, I do have a conscience. To allow the Benefactors to harvest humanity would be -- let's just say messy."

"Why do you need human specimens anyway?" Sandra asked Gladstone.

"Allow me to introduce you all to someone."

A leather-shrouded person wearing a full helmet arrived inside. Gladstone nodded to this person and he removed his helmet. This person's head seemed to be human and its skin a mixture of biological tissue with energy moving around it. It was dying. "This is one of the last residing members of the Benefactors," Gladstone said.

"Tell us more about them," Sandra asked.

"The Benefactors are cold, a race of hyper-evolved beings. They require pure human DNA to symbiotically join with them in order to survive. Your children will live enhanced, very fruitful lives that have a far greater longevity than yours," replied Gladstone. "The baby that you're carrying has some kind of augmented DNA. No doubt from an old friend of mine trying to make good."

Sandra became deeply concerned, "What do you mean? Is my baby okay?"

"It won't be if you give birth naturally. Augmented DNA must be monitored at all times."

"Okay, Gladstone! I'll give up my baby and I also give up my future children to you," she replied.

Rick felt as if he had just been struck by a thunderbolt. "Sandra, darling, you don't know what you're saying right now!"

"You heard him. The baby can't be born naturally, and anyway, it's a bit late for you to play the role of the concerned parent. It's the only way to save countless billions of lives and one very special one too."

"No way! I won't let you! I'll die before I let that happen!" Rick replied. "Don't you know that I would never give up a child of mine, no matter how enhanced they may become, to be slaves to aliens? It's my DNA, our children; I could never condemn them to such an existence! How could you even think this?"

"I always thought my children would do something profound, or at least I would guide them that way. Saving humanity is not the burden you're describing for them. Who's to say they would survive on Earth even if Moon X never appeared in the sky? Who's to say they wouldn't be killed by natural disasters, climate change, or nuclear war? Our child is a gift, a gift that will save the human race."

Gladstone smiled and said to Rick, "Passing the gift on, I like that. It seems your wife has an opposing view to yours, Rick. Very soon, their probe will arrive, you see, that's why this planetoid is regenerating, so it will be sufficiently capable of being detectable."

He then grabbed Seth by the neck. "But you knew all this, didn't you, Seth? Tell me, what else has my dear old friend, Fielding, told you?"

"I beat you before, Gladstone. I'll do it again!"

"No, I don't think you're going to get out of this one that easily."

Just then, Seth opened up his fist and threw a small sphere at Gladstone. It rolled over and over beside him. Gladstone laughed, and then it exploded!

"Rick, Sandra, come on!" Seth screamed.

They headed out through the smoke to the corridor. Rick helped Sandra to the jeep while Seth shot at the remaining guards. He made a run for it toward the jeep. He hopped inside it while Rick was at the driving seat; they drove off. As the jeep was traveling out of Capitol City, Seth became distracted as he heard Fielding's voice in his head yet again. "Seth! Seth!"

"Fielding's trying to tell me something! My brain's fried!" Seth cried.

"Concentrate, Seth! Ask him how do we destroy the probe?" Rick implored him.

"Fielding! A probe is coming to find this planetoid, ARRRGGGH!"

"SWIM, that's how, Seth. You have to use SWIM!" Fielding's voice answered.

And with that, Seth passed out.

"Seth! Seth!" Sandra said.

"We have to keep on moving!" Rick urged her.

Rick, Sandra, and Seth were at the location of Seth's shuttle where they landed when they first arrived on Moon X. It was a dry night, and the air had a saltiness to it, making Rick and Sandra thirsty. Seth was used to this. He was slightly delirious and being nursed by Sandra. Rick looked up the shuttle's computer system on SWIM. "Honey, I think I got something," he said to his wife. She moved over closer to her husband and watched the monitor. Rick continued, "SWIM means: Shock Wave Inversion Mechanism. It's a small subterranean station located in the core of Moon X."

"What does SWIM do?" asked Sandra.

"According to this, it creates the cloaking bubble around Moon X to hide it outside our normal space and time."

"We have no knowledge of how to operate it — just how are we going to use it to stop the probe?"

"We have to blow it up!" replied Rick tenaciously.

"What about us? We will blow ourselves up too!"

"Even if you could pilot this shuttle — you wouldn't make it in time. Not so long ago, you were willing to enslave our unborn child."

"That's a cheap shot. I was doing right for humanity also!"

"Blowing up this SWIM is the only way — I'd rather have my child never born than be enslaved!"

"Don't I get a say in this at all?"

"Just like you gave me a say with Gladstone earlier!" complained Rick, still trying to pull the proverbial knife from his back.

With that bickering, Seth became more lucid. "Shut up, you two! I know what to do!"

"Seth, are you alright?" Sandra asked him in a caring tone.

"I'll live. I know how to reprogram SWIM," he replied, then turned to Rick. "It doesn't have to be a cataclysmic event, Rick!"

"Glad to hear it," Sandra said.

"Okay, Seth. Let me guess, Fielding magically appeared to you and revealed where this station is?" Rick asked Seth.

"It's deep in Moon X's core."

"I know that already! Just how in the hell are we supposed to get down there?"

"Why, through the ocean, of course. You know, the one you've seen southernmost?"

"Oh, yeah. Sure, that one."

The shuttle once again left Moon X's upper atmosphere. The seemingly placid Earth and moon kept a waiting, watchful eye in the distant background. The Capitol City was now almost fully restored; time was running out. The probe became visible in the deepest reaches of the solar system. The shuttle veered to the south of Moon X toward its tiny ocean. Inside the shuttle, the control pads and computer systems began to fail. There were sparks and static everywhere.

"What's wrong? The ship's coming apart!" Rick said.

"The Benefactors' probe has entered the solar system. We must hurry!" Seth replied.

"Can't you zap it with something?" asked Sandra.

"No. I have no weapons. We're about to submerge!"

Seconds later, Seth's shuttle submerged with a forceful splash into Moon X's small but deep ocean. Rick, Sandra, and Seth saw from the shuttle's window the various alien underwater life forms. Sandra was mesmerized. "They're beautiful!"

"How far away is SWIM?" Rick asked Seth.

"Not far."

Seth's shuttle moved closer to an "X" shaped structure that was SWIM. They all saw the station from the main window. Moon X was moving closer to the moon.

CHAPTER 16

MEANWHILE, back on Earth in the observation room at Section-S, Spence and Hayes were witnessing these events on a large screen. There were also a small number of people and a supervisor present, monitoring the situation. There was a sense of panic in the room, as throughout the world. "I thought you said they weren't going to collide with each other?" Spence asked Hayes.

"I could never understand any of it!" Hayes replied in a dismal tone.

Spence quickly turned to Kimberly. "You! Explain this?"

"They're not! They each attract each other, and because their respective gravitational fields are fluctuating -- then they push each other away."

Back on Moon X in the shuttle, "That's SWIM," Seth said.

"Let's stop that probe!" Rick said, asserting his control over this very perplexing situation.

"I'm gonna try to log into SWIM's access codes," Seth said and began to tap numbers into the console in front of him. "INCORRECT ACCESS CODES" appeared on the screen.

"Damn it! Gladstone must have changed them!"

"Just what the hell do we do now? Is there any way you can bypass them?" Rick demanded.

"I'm afraid not. We've lost."

"Get us back to Gladstone now, Seth," Sandra implored Seth.

"Why, Sandra? What do you have in mind?" Rick asked her.

"Rick, we must give Gladstone our baby and future children. Don't you see that it's the only way we can save our own baby and other children in the world!" Sandra said, then she started experiencing a vision of a young teenager. Rick was oblivious to her experience. "Mom, I'm contacting you from the future. You must tell daddy not to kill Gladstone. He needs his DNA to reach the Benefactors. You must convince him this! And he's says, "Hi""

"My daughter. I'm so sorry, but how can I see you?"

"Gladstone's serum. He didn't realize he passed on the gift of precognition to you and I."

Sandra was about to ask her daughter her name when suddenly Seth's skin underwent a color change. He became almost dark grey in appearance. He tried to speak but was unable to.

"What's wrong with him?"

"It must be the concoction of sedatives that Doctor Snowdon gave him. He's poisoned," replied Rick.

"Rick?! You need Gladstone's DNA to save everyone. It's the only way to reason with the Benefactors."

"What?" he asked, confused.

"What are you doing?" Sandra yelled.

He didn't answer her; instead, he grabbed the controls and steered the shuttle toward SWIM. Seth's shuttle was on a direct collision course with it. Seth was bleeding and fell back onto Rick, resulting in him losing control of the vessel. As it veered on its wayward trajectory, the shuttle made impact with SWIM, followed by a large explosion.

In the observation room on Earth, the two moons were visible above them on this clear night, and on their LCD screens.

"They have failed! They didn't re-cloak Moon X! It's too late!" Spence cried.

"Damn them!" Hayes said to himself.

Seth was bleeding and fell back onto Rick. The shuttle, now

underwater, quickly crashed into SWIM, followed by a large explosion. Moon X vanished! It was just the regular moon orbiting the Earth once more.

Spence and Hayes had also just witnessed the sudden disappearance of Moon X on the large screen.

"They did it!" yelled Hayes.

"Thank God! I can't believe it!" Spence said to himself.

"Confirm that thing is gone!" Hayes ordered the supervisor.

The Supervisor checked and rechecked the data at his computer station and nodded. "Good. Well done, Rick!"

CHAPTER 17

IT WAS MUCH LATER. The location: the outskirts of Capital City. Rick was lying on the ground. There were remains of the shuttle pod everywhere. He tried to get up but had difficulty. He was in severe pain. He glanced around at the shuttle's debris and saw Seth's body. He forced himself upright and checked his surroundings. "Seth? Seth?"

He turned Seth over only to discover that he was dead. He stood up. "Sandra? Sandra?" he yelled.

"Over here, Rick!" she replied, faintly.

He walked quickly over to the opposite end of where he was. When he saw his wife, blood was coming out of her as if she had just suffered a terrible miscarriage. "Sandra, oh no!" he said, realizing his sacrifice.

"I think I lost the baby... I'm so sorry, Rick," she said sobbing.

He reached out and held her. "It's all my fault, honey... I shouldn't have fought you."

"Rick, darling... you have to make sure that Gladstone doesn't get to murder anybody else's babies! You can't let him destroy the world that our child would have called home!"

"Sandra, stay with me! Stay with me, honey!" he cried out.

Sandra closed her eyes and passed away. Rick stood up and roared with ferocious anger. Something suddenly caught his attention. It was the Earth. It was different in appearance and substance. It had rings around it like Saturn and appeared to have been ravaged by a powerful force. Something was very wrong with it. He moved over to the shuttle's rubble to find something with which he could dig two graves.

After Rick buried Sandra and Seth, he knelt and prayed over their graves. He never regarded himself as religious or pious in any way, but it felt like the right thing to do. He walked aimlessly in the direction of Capital City down a long road. Tears fell from his eyes. He had no idea how he was to proceed now, only to kill Gladstone. Suddenly, there was a slight distortion in front of him, and Fielding emerged! "Who are you?" he asked, startled.

"My name is Fielding. Are you Seth Odyssey?"

"No, Seth's dead along with my wife and unborn child. All in the name of your private war with Gladstone!"

"I'm so sorry you got caught up in all of this. It was my intention to have Seth topple Gladstone. I see the planetoid has returned. Are you from the other side?"

"'Other side', what do you mean?"

"Seth activated SWIM to traverse this entire rock from one universe to another. Your universe, your Earth, which is not that you see now."

"I thought it was cloaked outside of space and time?"

"That's all Seth knew. Only Gladstone and I knew the terrible truth -- welcome to your mirror universe, Rick."

"Wait, I must admit I know about as much about quantum physics as the next guy, but how's that even scientifically possible?"

"It's quite simple, really. That SWIM station you blew up was keeping a lid on a very old, decaying black hole -- a very small, miniature black hole. This singularity is unique; however, instead of sucking in light and matter, it emits negative energy. SWIM harnessed and controlled this energy. Every molecule on Moon X and every molecule in every person on it were enveloped by this energy that 'pulled' it and everyone into your universe. Do you understand now?"

"I think so. What happened to your Earth?"

"The Benefactors ravaged this Earth a long time ago. That's why I set up a colony here to appease them, only Gladstone had other ideas. He needs to be stopped before the same occurs on your Earth."

"Don't you think I know that already -- but I need your help! Seth's dead, I've no weapons!"

"I'll help you. Together we must go to what from your point of view is the mirror Earth."

"Look at it. Can it support life?"

"Just barely enough. I'll provide you with a protective suit. Come, my home isn't far."

"Can I ask you a question, Mr. Fielding?"

"Go right ahead."

"Why did you pretend to be dead all this time?"

"I needed a younger man. Old age is disadvantageous at most."

It was dusk. Rick found this universe to be eerie and formidable. Both he and Fielding arrived at what appeared to be a shack of rubble. Fielding gestured to Rick to pull over a large sheet of metal that was concealing an entrance. Both men went inside. It was Fielding's home, and its simplistic design surprised Rick. There was a computer system like the ones he had seen earlier on Moon X. Fielding walked over to a compartment. "I'll get that suit -- the atmosphere will burn you if you don't wear it."

He pulled its door open. Rick moved over to him and took one of the two suits with helmets. "Just what the hell am I supposed to do when I go to the mirror Earth?"

"I'll instruct you step by step by a com link when you get down there. I see you were quite adept at piloting Seth's shuttle."

"I managed."

"Wait until you see mine."

Fielding directed him beyond the room where the lighting revealed a sleek shuttle craft.

"Has it weapons? I need weapons."

"Oh, yes. Quite a vast complement too."

Rick walked around the vessel, inspecting it.

"It can fly twice as fast and the flight plan for your destination and back has been pre-programmed," Fielding continued.

"Tell me what makes you different from Gladstone? How do I know that I can trust you?"

"My personal beliefs, my core moral being is bound by what I think are the governing laws of the universe. I know there is a powerful energy that represents all that is good, and there has to be an equal energy that is dark."

"Karma, sort of."

"Yes, Rick. I'm aware of the word and yes, you could describe what I certainly know in my heart to be like that. Gladstone, on the other hand, is a cold, hard scientist that I once rejected his theories. Ever since, he's been trying to prove me wrong."

"You differed in how to help the Benefactors?"

"They're dying. My plan was to enlist volunteers from this Earth, my home, and with their fullest cooperation, save the Benefactors from extinction. Gladstone wants to prove me wrong. The man can't simply take rejection at any level... do you trust me?"

"You know, I came here with my wife and friend to prevent our own moon and Moon X from causing havoc on Earth. I wish it were as simple as preventing something probably unlikely as that. What's not to trust? Hayes or anybody at home would never dream of such a thing that's taking place on this rock. Let's not waste any more time! I've got to save the day!"

Fielding's shuttle took off without any problems. Rick had been given a quick course in piloting instruction and was at the helm. It soon left Moon X's atmosphere, heading toward the mirror Earth. Rick, attired in the protective suit, was wearing the helmet also. He was blocking out his grief by demanding himself to complete this mission. He could hear his wife's dying last words still telling him to save humanity. He pushed the comm. button to communicate with Fielding, who was still on Moon X.

"Sanchez, here. I'll be entering the upper atmosphere momentarily, standby..."

As Fielding began to speak back to him, Rick and his shuttle manoeuvred around the mirror version of New York City, "Okay Sanchez. Stick to the flight plan's trajectory. You should be on a direct course to this Earth's version of New York City. When you reach there, slow down and keep flying till you see a large emitter array."

Located in Central Park and dominating the local skyline, Rick's shuttle swerved around it like a honeybee. "Fielding, it's gigantic! Doesn't seem to be operational though?"

"Trust me -- it's operational."

"What do you want me to do with it, apart from a direct collision course, we're gonna need some ammo to blow it up?"

As Rick's shuttle left the vicinity of the emitter array, he was zapped by a similar craft. He was still alive and knew he had been hit. He tried to steer his vessel away from crashing into the ravaged and derelict skyscrapers. He managed to veer the shuttle into the river.

There was a large alien chamber located on this Earth's equivalent of Central Park, composed of a mixture of organic matter and light. Inside this chamber, the Alien Being whom Rick and Sandra first saw on Moon X entered. He was holding a mechanical device which he communicated with by speaking into it, and his voice came out in English. This was to facilitate Gladstone, who was also present.

"Our probe has identified another Earth for us to harvest," this mechanical-sounding voice said.

"There's no need, Your Excellency. My original plan can still provide you with high-grade specimens," Gladstone replied.

Suddenly everyone and everything became distorted like a rippling effect in space and time.

"What was that?" Gladstone asked.

"My race is ascertaining that right now. On the subject at hand, you have failed us, Gladstone. You allowed one of your mere subjects to eliminate the entire crop; however, fortunately, this person has revealed another source for us."

"It is my strongest belief that my theories on selective reproduction and eugenics are the only solution to your requirements."

"We captured this human. Bring in the human."

Two of Gladstone's guards escorted Rick into the center of the chamber. "This human is guilty of destroying the entire harvest. Perhaps he has qualities that you, Gladstone, are obviously deficient in," the Alien Being continued.

"No! No! First of all, this is not the same human. I saw the dead remains of the one you're talking about and second, he is an inferior human from the other side."

"This 'inferior human' successfully managed to evade you on several occasions and found himself here."

"I said I saw the remains of his friend, Seth Odyssey; I also managed to extract something from this man here, Rick Sanchez, his pregnant woman."

"Speak without riddles, Gladstone!"

Gladstone snapped his fingers, and his remaining guard entered carrying something in the form of a transparent bio-container containing the embryo of Sandra's baby.

"This is his unborn daughter. When she matures, I can mate with her myself to produce more than adequate offspring," Gladstone replied.

Revulsion consumed Rick. He charged at Gladstone, roaring, "Never!!!" However, he was stunned by the guard's weapon. Suddenly, Fielding appeared and fired on the two guards. Gladstone pulled out his dagger with a smile of perverse satisfaction. "It's been a long time, Fielding."

He then charged at Fielding. Rick was now awake and was slowly recomposing himself. Fielding fired his weapon at Gladstone, but it had zero effect on him. Gladstone moved menacingly, slowly toward Fielding. He began to wave his dagger side to side, enjoying the fact that he was going to kill his prey. Gladstone turned around and saw Rick. Rick assumed a belligerent posture and charged at him. Gladstone raised his right arm to punch Rick. He was successful and managed to push Rick a few meters back. Rick was not backing off; instead, he charged at his nemesis with prevailing vengeful force. Gladstone was jilted. Fielding moved over to the dagger's location and picked it up. Rick yet again charged at Gladstone. They exchanged punches. Gladstone kicked Rick in the stomach. He was winded. "You see, Rick. You can't beat me!" Gladstone cried.

"Bring it on, Gladstone!"

They exchanged more punches, kicks, and exotic rhythms of fighting.

"Here Rick! Catch!" Fielding yelled.

Fielding flung the dagger to Rick, and as it flew through the air, Gladstone managed to catch it first. "Goodbye, Rick!" he said.

Gladstone was about to stab Rick when Fielding fired his weapon at the dagger; it fell to the ground. Gladstone was now thrown off guard. Rick noticed this and seized the opportunity. He grabbed the dagger off Gladstone and was about to stab him in the heart. "Wait, Sandra told me that I would need something from you to end this." Gladstone didn't know what he was talking about, and he was subdued, Fielding rushed over to Rick. "Rick, are you alright?"

"I think you better lock him up somewhere good."

"That's exactly what I will do, Rick."

Fielding and Rick tied up Gladstone and threw the dagger away from him. The Alien Being moved over to Rick and Fielding. "We, the Benefactors, wish to negotiate."

"I want that container that's keeping my daughter's embryo alive," Rick said.

Fielding went over to the far end of the chamber and took the bio-container off its stand. He then carried it over to Rick. Rick stared at it, tears falling from his eyes.

"Rick, I am familiar with Gladstone's technology. I know

how to keep the embryo alive and bring your daughter to life through normal gestation. You see, I studied your world and chose you and Sandra so I could augment the DNA when you both conceived this child," Fielding said.

"What do you mean?"

"I monitored your coupling with Sandra. Do you wish me to proceed?"

"I would like that," Rick replied graciously.

"These ripple effects in space-time that we're all feeling are caused by the destruction of SWIM. With SWIM gone, there is no longer a means to invert the shock waves emanating from the decaying black hole. We must find another way to regulate them, otherwise, they could cause untold damage to both realities," the Alien Being said with strong urgency.

"You seem to know a lot about this. Just what kind of damage are you talking about?" Fielding asked.

"Our analysis has shown us that the same radiation Seth used to murder everybody on Moon X is leaking from the decaying black hole. That's why we built and designed SWIM in the first place—to regulate this radiation."

Rick paused for a moment, then experienced a realization. "There must be some kind of bargaining chip we can use with your people?" he asked the Alien Being.

The Alien Being was silent, then: "That is a most intriguing idea, if not a perplexing one at that. Just what would you want in return?"

"To leave my Earth, humanity as I know it, alone," Rick replied.

"Yes. We could agree to such a treaty."

"Wait! Wait! How are we going to achieve this? We're better off building SWIM again!" Fielding warned.

"No. We don't have enough time for that. Rick's way is the only way, and we believe we have a means to achieve this," the Alien Being replied.

"Very well."

"How?" Rick asked.

"If you must become one with us. You could enter our domain with the embryo. You see, our natural habitat is the ring of energy surrounding this planet. Your consciousness could be allowed to exist here for a short period, and more importantly, we will get to know your species' baser instincts free from intellectual pollution when they are in their infancy."

"Is that even possible?"

"Yes, if we only knew how to make you capable of separating your consciousness. You see, I appear to you now as a physical being, a corporeal representation of my essence. We need to make you the same as I."

"Wait, my wife told me before she died that I would require Gladstone's DNA if I was to meet your people face to face," implored Rick.

Fielding paused for a moment and experienced a realization. "That's right! His augmented DNA enabled him to see these aliens. I could extract some from his body and infuse with your own, Rick. That should do it."

The Alien Being nodded his head in agreement. Fielding wasted no time extracting a blood sample from Gladstone's body and injected Rick. Gladstone retaliated and managed to unravel his restraints. He was about to pick up his dagger. Rick quickly saw what he was trying to do and kicked the dagger toward Fielding. Fielding picked up it back up and thrust it through Gladstone's heart. He roared with the pain and fell back. Rick checked his pulse. "He's dead."

Fielding reacted with intense delight and then handed Rick a bio canister containing his unborn child's embryo. "Rick, you need to hold is; it's your daughter."

CHAPTER 18

RICK WAS STANDING UPRIGHT in the alien alcove, holding the canister that contained his and Sandra's daughter's embryo. It filled with bright light, which had no discomforting effects on his eyes. He had cybernetic enhancements attached to his body. His skin pigment was changing. He closed his eyes and drifted away somewhere else. The rippling effects through space and time were becoming more frequent. Each time this happened, the ring surrounding the mirror Earth's equator became more effulgent. Gladstone's former guards began adjusting the array as Fielding ordered them. He was helping the Alien Being with Rick's transformation. Rick had successfully transported his consciousness to the realm of the Benefactors, where it was comprised of white-coloured energy waves that appeared dull. Human faces began to emerge from these energy waves and converge around Rick and the canister containing the embryo's energy, and he could perceive them so. They spoke to him: "Why are you here? How did you enter our domain?" they demanded as one angry chorus.

"I come in peace, in search for peace," Rick replied.

"Your presence here has infected our realm."

A scanning ethereal wave of energy surrounded the canister. Then vehemently, an angry chorus yelled and demanded, "Be gone and never come back, or there will be consequences for your kind!"

"Please! Your kind needs our help. Surely there must be a way to solve your problems and both of our problems together?"

"We scanned the infant's mind. It's primitive and will ultimately be the undoing of our kind. Why would we want to work with an inferior species like humans? We only require one aspect of your pitiful existence."

"You won't even get that! Gladstone promised you perfect minds for your longevity—the decaying black hole is giving off dangerous radiation to humans that will cause them all to die."

"We built a means to control this radiation."

"SWIM is destroyed! You don't have the time to build another. Please, there has to be another way?!"

The faces began to encircle Rick. "We have analysed your mental patterns and determined that it was indeed you who destroyed SWIM. You are devious."

"Yes, I did. I had to. Gladstone was going to use my wife for genetic experiments. If I knew then the consequences, I would have done things differently," replied Rick with regret and sorrow.

The faces began to distort and quiver. "What are you doing to us?! Stop this now!"

"I am not doing anything!"

They became more distorted, forming and then reforming again. "Please! We beg you!"

"What's wrong with you? What are you feeling? That's it, you're all feeling!

"Yes... your emotions. They extend from joyous to unpleasant."

"Okay... it's not something that I can control too well. My emotions can get the better of me sometimes."

"They are quite tantalizing and appealing. We wish to experience this again and more."

"Okay again. Just one condition though..."

"Name it?"

"Leave my world alone!"

"Agreed. We will be in touch through our representative on your side. You are free to go."

Rick opened his eyes as Fielding helped him out of the alcove.

"Rick, are you alright?" he asked.

"Yeah, I think so. You know, up until now the Benefactors were only capable of experiencing cold, sterile mental logic. Now I have managed somehow to show them how to bridge the gap between the cerebral and emotional…"

Rick began breathing heavily. Fielding was concerned. "I think he's had enough."

The alien representative turned to Fielding, "Yes. His work is done here. My people have confirmed this new peace agreement between the humans and the Benefactors. This man named Rick enabled us to experience the emotional spectrum which in turn gave us the ability to imagine. We can solve our mutual problems through new perspectives of thought."

Three days later, Rick lay on a bed convalescing. His cybernetic enhancements had been removed. Fielding was also present. Rick opened his eyes. He was lucid.

"Rick, are you alright?" he asked him while tending to his scars.

"Yes, I think so."

He tried to get up.

"No, no, Rick. Rest for a little."

"It was like nothing I'd ever experienced before. Before my consciousness entered the ring, their realm, it was a dull grey haze. I connected with their thoughts, felt my emotions. They did the same. I showed them how to 'feel' again. This dull grey haze became awash with bright, pulsating colours that scintillated not only their minds but their hearts. We now have peace."

"When you're stronger, I'll get you back home."

Nine months later, Rick was now fully better. He was looking at the remains of the mirror version of his city. Fielding joined him.

"Did everything go smoothly?" Rick asked him.

"Yes, very much so."

A woman carrying a newborn baby girl arrived over to them.

"Congratulations, Rick. You're now a proud father of this beautiful baby girl," Fielding said.

Tears fell from Rick's eyes as he took his daughter from the woman. "Thank you for everything, Mister Fielding."

"Thank you, Rick, for ending the quagmire that almost destroyed us all."

"What are you going to do now?"

"There are still some survivors left on this earth. I intend to find them and give them a life worth living."

"Best of luck!"

"Now, how do I get home?"

"Follow me..."

Rick, carrying his baby daughter, followed Fielding down a laneway. They quickly entered a small nearby forest. There was another laneway. Rick continued to follow Fielding. The baby started to cry. Rick soothed her by giving her a pacifier. "Where exactly are you taking us?"

"Trust me, it's not that far from here," replied Fielding.

They suddenly heard shuffling amongst the trees. Fielding gestured to Rick not to react. "Who's that?"

Just then, three people emerged from the trees. They seemed hungry and were wearing shabby clothes. Fielding gently moved over near them and began to speak softly, "They're the survivors that I told you about, my people... Don't be afraid... I can provide you with food and shelter. We have achieved peace now. I'll be back to you as soon as I send this man and his daughter home."

The survivors were fretful but understood Fielding. He began walking ahead down the laneway. Rick, still carrying his daughter, followed him.

They arrived at Fielding's desired destination. It was a strange stone structure.

"Rick, we're here."

"What's this? How is this going to get me and my baby home?"

"Come closer... look through the center of the structure..."

Rick carried out his request and handed the baby gently to Fielding, then moved nearer the structure. He began to peer at the center of it. Rick immediately saw a mirror reflection of Central Park, *our* earth's Central Park. There were people walking, a man jogging, and a couple seated on a bench. "This is the means by which I was able to bring Gladstone here from your earth," explained Fielding.

"Did you create this?"

"No, this has always been here. I'm not sure for how long."

"The opening is tiny. Just how are we going to fit through?"

Fielding took out a small device from his jacket pocket. "Here, stand back, Rick."

Rick backed away and took the baby from him. Fielding activated the device, and it began to emit a laser beam. He focused the beam at the portal, and it expanded to become much larger.

"Go now, Rick. Your work is done here!"

Rick, holding his daughter, walked into the portal. Next, he saw everything he had seen in the stone structure's reflection, but it was reality. It was as if to the people in Central Park, Rick and the baby appeared from thin air. These people were mesmerized. Rick and his daughter were now back home.

CHAPTER 19

THE DUSKY SKY IN WASHINGTON, DC was dominated by one single moon again -- our moon. There was a slight dust cloud where Moon X would be, where it once was. Inside the Pentagon, it was just Secretary Spence and Hayes who were present, and they seemed bewildered at the ever-perplexing situation of moons appearing and disappearing without anyone knowing just what had really happened in the mirror earth. Spence couldn't accept that Moon X was gone for good. It was coming up to an election, and he needed a much better explanation, any explanation other than his own simple conjecture. "You mean to tell me Moon X has vanished for good?" he asked Hayes.

"That's what it looks to the naked eye as well as our orbital satellites. It has been almost ten months since it went back to wherever it came from. Three of our best gone with it. I wouldn't mind if I wasn't particularly too hard on Sanchez. He was an exemplary agent."

"And the risk of alien invasion?"

"Negligible. Moon X is no longer an instrument to achieve that anymore."

"I wonder where it went to."

"Probably back to where that abomination came from. I

think we should honour our three agents with a hero's day commemoration."

"Agreed. They saved the world, that's if this is all over."

As Spence uttered those words, the phone rang. Hayes quickly picked up the receiver and could see the dreading expression on Spence's face, who rushed to the window to gaze up at the sky to see if his long-lost enemy had come back. Hayes also watched the sky through the large windows, only the sky was empty apart from planes flying as normal. "Hayes here, what?! You mean they're back? What, just him? I want him debriefed as soon as he is checked out."

"What's going on, Hayes?"

"Sanchez is back. He lost his wife, and Northington's gone too. He is joined by his baby daughter."

"That's interesting," he replied, looking up at the sky again.

It was one week later. Rick had gone through medical examinations, physical and mental, as well as endless debriefings. He was now at the Pentagon in Spence's office and joined by Hayes. Rick knew they didn't believe him, and the story that he had to make up to hold the agreement he made with the Benefactors was not going to be palatable with Spence and Hayes. He knew he had to sell his lies harder. "As I said, it's over."

"Your report, to say the least, is quite vague. Just how did you manage to persuade the Benefactors from harvesting our world?" Spence asked.

"As I've already said, they saw my sheer brutality when I murdered Gladstone. They were put off by us."

"Ah, yes. The mysterious Gladstone. The so-called 'superhuman.'"

"Yes?"

"You stated in your report that he was going to mate with your daughter when she was of child-rearing age?"

"Where is all this going? I've already told you everything."

"It's my job to see if you have not been coerced in any way. For all we know, you could be setting us up by doing recon for these 'Benefactors.'"

"Secretary Spence, use your infamous interrogation methods on me if you wish! I have not been 'coerced' in any way, I can assure you!"

"We will be watching you."

Rick got up and left. He knew that was his cue to leave from Spence. Hayes just watched. He knew that he had now always underestimated Rick right from the start and was not only feeling a little remorseful but also foolish.

SIXTEEN YEARS later on a spring afternoon in Rivers Town, Rick was joined by his now-teenaged daughter. He was relaxing outside his back garden, having a few beers. This had become his new routine since he retired from the FBI two months previously. His career from the point he returned to this earth was normal, boring in fact. It all seemed like a dream, those interstellar adventures and crossing the boundaries between realities, not to mention moons popping out here and there – well, one that was called Moon X. He never heard from Fielding again and often pondered whether he was still alive. He felt nostalgic for that time and sad because it was where he lost Sandra over his own pig-headedness. He often asked himself if he wasn't so caught up in his stubbornness in not trying to meet her halfway and somehow finding a compromise. He knew he shouldn't have blown up SWIM. That's what killed Sandra and Seth but also solved the problem with the Benefactors. He was thinking, surely it could have ended better for everyone.

"Wendy, it's time I told you what really happened to your mother. You're old enough to understand now," he told his daughter.

"It's got to do with that other moon that was once in the sky? Did I come from there? Are you my real father?"

"Of course, I am, and never doubt that. But yes, it's got to do with Moon X. Your mother lost her life there. I buried her on it, not knowing you were still alive. It was only until someone else, whose intentions were dishonourable, who saved you, and for that, I'm truly grateful."

"This person was the bad guy called Gladstone, right?"

"I'm afraid so. I almost allowed you to die."

"I forgive you, Dad. It's not like you did anything intentionally bad to me. I wish that I could have known my mother."

"First, you must do something for her. This Gladstone altered both of your respective DNA strands which made you both able to communicate with each other. I must point out that this only happened just once ever. When you see her, don't be scared as there's something very crucial that you must tell her to tell me. It's got to do with Gladstone, his own DNA. You have to say that I need it to meet the Benefactors. Oh, and tell her, I said "Hi"."

Wendy was surprised and feeling apprehensive about firstly experiencing some kind of strange vision and secondly that vision being her deceased mother. "I need to know her, Dad. Please tell me all you know about her."

"I'll tell you all about her starting now. She was beautiful, intelligent, but also highly ethical. More ethical than I ever was."

He began telling her at this moment all he knew about his wife, her mother. Wendy listened with wonder and began to stare at the sky above, knowing her mother lay at rest somewhere long away and so unattainable, yet so near.

THE END

ABOUT THE AUTHOR

 John Paul Warren was born on June 12, 1975 in Ireland. He writes passionately in his free time about characters who are pulled into ethical dilemmas and use personal introspection to solve their problems and usually references on our ever so strange human condition.

To learn more about John P. Warren and discover more Next Chapter authors, visit our website at www.nextchapter.pub.

Moon X
ISBN: 978-4-82418-998-1

Published by
Next Chapter
2-5-6 SANNO
SANNO BRIDGE
143-0023 Ota-Ku, Tokyo
+818035793528

7th January 2024